The radio crackled. He grabbed it out of his pocket. "Ryan Nichols here."

"It's Mike, Ryan. Heard your call. Just coming out of Jamestown Bay. I'm on my way. Slow going, but hang on, kids; we'll be there in less than two hours."

Ryan looked at Laurette. He didn't know if it was rain or tears on her cheeks. Probably a mix. "Could you hear?"

She shook her head.

"Mike's on his way," he shouted.

She waved at the water, rocks, and surf around them. "Can we hold out until he gets here?" she yelled into the wind.

"All things are possible with God. We'll let Him navigate for us." He thought he saw a slight smile curve her lips. "Rette, try to move around a little. You need to keep your circulation going. Stomp your feet."

"I can't feel them." She tried to stand but grabbed the seat when the boat rocked to one side. She fell into the seat by the wheel. "Are you warm?" she shouted at him.

He patted his mustang suit. "That's what this thing is for. We need to get you one."

She nodded and laid her head back against the seat.

Ryan alternately watched her and where the boat was drifting. Was she asleep? How advanced was the hypothermia? He longed to hold her, but she was better off under the shelter provided by the canvas top than at the stern with him. *Please, Lord, take care of her.*

It seemed like an eternity before the shape of the tugboat appeared in the clouds that met the sea.

MARILOU H. FLINKMAN and her husband have retired to a home in Arizona. Since the Kairos Prison Ministry is not active in Arizona, Marilou has become a food bank volunteer. She says she has finally gotten out of prison but the Lord has found another way for her to serve. She is active in her church in Chandler. The Flinkmans enjoy travel. They have explored the backcountry of Brazil, gone on safaris in Kenya and Tanzania, and been in Hong Kong, and recently returned from Russia. Marilou is an avid reader and enjoys visiting the couple's six children and thirteen grandchildren and fishing in Alaska. To find out how Marilou is currently involved, please visit her Web site at www.marilouflinkman.com.

Books by Marilou H. Flinkman

A note from the Author:
I love to hear from my readers! You may correspond with me by writing:

Marilou H. Flinkman
Author Relations
PO Box 719
Uhrichsville, OH 44683

ISBN 1-59310-608-4

ALASKAN SUMMER

Our mission is to publish and distribute inspirational products offering exceptional value and biblical encouragement to the masses.

All of the characters and events in this book are fictitious. Any resemblance to actual persons, living or dead, or to actual events is purely coincidental.

All scripture quotations are taken from the King James Version of the Bible.

PRINTED IN THE U.S.A.

one

The flight from Seattle had been uneventful and the scenery spectacular. Laurette kept her nose close to the window as the panorama of the Canadian Rockies held her in awe. Snowcapped peaks seemed to touch the sky; glaciers and glistening mountain lakes beckoned to her then disappeared beneath a layer of clouds as the plane approached Sitka, Alaska.

Laurette felt the small aircraft bank and turn, descending into the clouds below. Gripping the armrests, she tensed when the pilot announced he would make one more attempt to land as the plane changed altitude again. "If there is no break in the cloud cover, we will go on to Juneau," he said.

Heaving a huge sigh, Laurette wondered why she had let Jenny talk her into this. Her college roommate had lived in Sitka for several years before her father retired from the Coast Guard. Jenny had coaxed Laurette into applying for a job with Southeast Alaska Maritime, the port agent serving cruise ships and their passengers' myriad needs while they were in Sitka. Laurette closed her eyes and said a quick prayer for Jenny's father. His heart attack had sent her roommate rushing to his side.

The plane dived, throwing Laurette forward against her seat belt. Her eyes popped open and her prayer rapidly changed to "Lord Jesus, please keep us safe." All she could see now were clouds rushing past her window. She repeated her prayer like a mantra until the view cleared and she felt the wheels bouncing on the runway. At least she thought it was ground. Whichever window she looked out, she saw only water. Her heart continued to beat out a rapid rhythm.

By the time the steward opened the door, Laurette felt back in control. She squared her shoulders, pulled her backpack from the overhead bin, and followed the other passengers off the plane. In the terminal she spotted a tall, thin, but athletic-looking young man holding a sign with her name printed in large black letters. *This is the welcoming committee?* she wondered, seeing his glum expression. Aside from that, he wasn't bad to look at. His dark hair looked like it had been combed by the wind. He wore pressed jeans and a jacket with the Southeast Alaska Maritime logo.

Hiding her apprehension, Laurette picked her way through the small crowd of passengers to reach the man with the sign. "Hi. I'm Laurette Martel." *He must be over six foot,* she thought, offering him her hand.

He raised an eyebrow and gave her a crooked smile. His blue eyes showed no warmth when he touched her hand. "Welcome to Sitka. I'm Ryan Nichols. Do you have luggage?"

"Yes. Jenny gave me a long list of things I would need. I'm sorry she couldn't come."

"Me, too."

Laurette wondered at his tone. Jenny had never mentioned any particular guy, but it seemed Ryan knew her—and was apparently very disappointed.

"Luggage is this way."

She scurried to keep up with his long stride. "Mr. Personality," she said under her breath.

As soon as she saw her big duffel bag, she grabbed it off the carousel. She'd barely put it down when the large cardboard box she had checked appeared. Ryan saw her reach for it and managed to snag the awkward package before she could react.

"The company van is parked out front. I'll carry the box. Follow me." Her official greeter grabbed the box and started for the door.

"Thanks," she said as she slung on her backpack and picked up the duffel bag. "Another adventure," she muttered, hurrying after his retreating figure.

When he shoved the box in the back of the van and reached for her duffel bag, she warned him, "My laptop is in my backpack. I'd like to keep it up front."

Again he arched one bushy eyebrow and said, "Suit yourself."

He eased the van away from the airport and drove across a long bridge, giving Laurette a little time to look around. She realized now that the runway her plane had landed on was on a narrow—or was *the* narrow—strip of land on what she assumed was an island, since she hadn't paid much attention to that part of the map. Ryan spoke just as she opened her mouth to ask.

"You have a place to stay in Sitka?"

"I made a reservation at a place called Edith's Bed-and-Breakfast on Monastery Street. Looks like I can walk to work from there, according to my map." Laurette ducked when a small plane took off from the water and roared over the van.

"Seaplanes have the right-of-way here. Boats have to make room for them," he said, gesturing toward the water where the various crafts had indeed given the seaplane a wide berth. "You'll get used to it."

He sounds like a really bored tour guide. "Nice to know." She took note of the many fishing boats moored in the harbor.

"We'll stop by the office first. The boss will want to meet you."

"Fine," she said, looking at the sights and ignoring her less than friendly driver. The clouds still hovered over the city but did not blot out the faint shadow of the surrounding mountains.

"You handled that luggage with no problem. You'll be doing a lot of that now."

Laurette did not know how to answer him. She just

looked at his profile and wondered if that was meant to be a compliment. "I grew up on a farm. I'm used to hard work," she said firmly.

He smiled at her. *He could be good looking if he did that more often,* she thought. Her thoughts were interrupted as he pulled into a large parking lot.

Ryan pointed to the building near a dock. "That's the Centennial Building. The dock below it is where the tenders bring people off the ships. The cruise ships anchor out there in Crescent Bay."

Laurette was not about to admit she had no idea what a *tender* could be. Beyond the dock she saw several pleasure crafts in the harbor. She scurried to keep up with Ryan when he got out of the van. They jaywalked across the street and went up some stairs next to a souvenir shop. He led her past a couple of closed doors to the end of the hall. Here, the door stood open, and a man in his midthirties turned to greet her.

"Welcome, Laurette. Glad to have you here."

She shook his proffered hand.

"I'm Tyler Healy. Do you go by Laurette?"

"Yes, sir, but my father calls me Rette," she answered politely, wondering why she'd added something so irrelevant.

"I go by Tyler. Not very formal here." His welcome warmed Laurette. Her boss wasn't as tall as Ryan, but since she stood only five feet four inches, she looked up to almost everyone. Tyler had sandy-colored hair and a neatly trimmed beard. He wore a long-sleeved sport shirt and dark blue jeans. She spotted a sport coat on the back of a chair. She wondered if her own slacks and sweater looked travel worn. *Can't be helped,* she said silently, finger-combing her curly hair.

"Do you have a place to stay tonight?" he asked. "My wife said to bring you home if you didn't."

"Thank you for the invitation, but I made a reservation at Edith's B and B. I'll have to find a permanent place and a vehicle to drive soon."

"We'll start on that tomorrow. Right now, let me show you around the office. Would you like a cup of coffee?"

She took the offered drink. It was strong and bitter. *Must be Alaskan style.* She sipped the dark brew as she followed Tyler. Laurette realized Ryan had left them without comment. There were three rooms with desks and machines. The fax machine started to clack. He picked up the message being sent.

"This is usually how the cruise ship captains contact us. They let us know what they'll need while they're in port, and we do our best to take care of them." He turned to a cabinet. "Let me give you a cell phone. Be sure to keep it charged and turned on at all times. This is how we stay in contact."

Laurette took the phone. She turned as Ryan appeared in the doorway. "Could you find a VHF radio for Laurette?" Tyler asked him. "We don't use them often, but they're a backup if the ships are out of cell phone range," he explained to her. "Your call name will be SAM 3. I'm SAM 1 and Ryan is SAM 2," her new boss instructed. "Bring an extra battery pack, too," he called to the departing Ryan.

She smiled. "Easy to remember." Laurette looked for a place to put her cup when Ryan came back with her radio and battery pack; she already had the phone in her other hand. "I left my backpack in the van." She put the cup on the windowsill and murmured, "Sorry. Don't have enough hands."

"Have we got a coat small enough?" Tyler asked Ryan. "You'll need the uniform and the pockets," he told Laurette with a smile.

"Uniform?" she questioned.

"We aren't in dress blues." He laughed. "We try to look presentable, particularly when we go aboard the ships. A good pair of jeans will do, and the company windbreaker will identify you as one of our employees."

Ryan came back with a jacket. "Smallest we've got."

She put down the phone and radio before pulling it on. "It fits okay," she announced, pushing the elastic in the cuffs up her wrists to keep the sleeves from falling over her hands. Next she stowed the phone and radio in the pockets and picked up her cup of coffee.

Through all this, Ryan hadn't spoken. Tyler didn't seem to notice, so Laurette tried not to show her discomfort with her coworker's obvious disapproval. Or was it her own self-consciousness?

She sat down in the chair by Tyler's desk while they chatted about Sitka and what would be expected of her.

"Do you have a church preference?" Tyler asked her.

"My family went to a community church near our ranch. In college I've been attending Grace Church. Kind of an evangelical service." The change in subject startled her.

Tyler beamed. "My wife and I belong to an evangelical congregation. Perhaps you'd like to join us on Sunday."

"I would like that," she answered, surprised to see Ryan slouch even farther down the wall he leaned against.

Doesn't look like Mr. Grouch is a believer, she thought. *Don't make snap judgments, Rette. Maybe he just goes to a different church and—*

"Only one ship in port today. Season is just starting," Tyler explained, interrupting her thoughts. "By the end of May, we'll have ships daily. Why don't you take off, Ryan? Leave early while you can. Could you drop Laurette off at Edith's on your way home?"

"Sure." The young man stood up. "I think we can get her luggage into my car."

Tyler laughed. "You might have to throw out some of the garbage." His smile broadened. "Ryan has a drinking problem."

A shock wave hit as Laurette looked at her coworker.

Tyler continued to chuckle. "He's addicted to chocolate milk. The back of that little car of his is usually piled up with empty cartons."

Ryan looked up with a sheepish grin. "Hey, Boss, you're making me look bad. I'm sure I can get Miss Martel and her luggage to Edith's B and B without any difficulty."

❧

Ryan led Laurette to a beat-up Volkswagen. "We'll pick up your stuff," he said as he opened the passenger door for her. He drove to where he'd parked the company van and stopped behind it, then went to open the back door.

"Let me help." She jumped out of the car.

"That's okay," he said, pushing her seat forward so he could load the box into the back of the VW. He piled the duffel bag on top of it. "Can you hold this in your lap?" he asked as he handed her the backpack.

"Sure." Laurette squeezed into the passenger seat with her pack.

"How come Jenny didn't come with you?" he asked, pulling out of the parking lot.

"Her father had a heart attack. She went to help her mother take care of him. Did you know her?"

"We went to the same school. She's younger than I am, but I saw her around."

"We were roommates in college. Jenny has another year to go."

Ryan didn't answer her. His thoughts went to the tall, willowy blond he had expected to work with this summer. They had dated a few times before her family moved. He sighed and looked at the petite girl clutching her backpack on her lap. She had a pert face with a cap of chestnut-colored curls. Her light brown eyes sparkled with excitement. *Kind of cute*, he thought.

"Is that Swan Lake?" she asked, pointing out the window.

"Yes. Have you been to Sitka before?"

"No. I just read all I could find out about the place. Got a map off the Internet so I won't get lost."

"That'll help," he said as much to himself as to her. *She can handle big bags and maybe find her way back to the airport. We can start her out hauling passenger luggage.* Ryan stopped the VW in front of the B and B. "Here we are."

"Thanks for the ride, Ryan. I can take that." She grabbed the duffel bag Ryan pulled out of the backseat, and he noticed she already had the pack on her back so her arms were free.

"I'll take the box in for you," he offered.

"I forgot to ask what time I should be at work," she said as they approached the door.

Her stricken look made him smile. "You'll get used to checking the schedule. We have to be available when the ships anchor. Show up at eight in the morning."

Edith greeted them and told Ryan where to put the bags and box. When he introduced Laurette, she greeted Edith politely and openly admired the decor. It looked cluttered with lace and bric-a-brac to Ryan. He beat a hasty retreat.

Wonder how long the good cheer will last, he thought, remembering Laurette's smiling face. *Hope that enthusiasm will keep her going for long hours and through lots of bad weather.*

He waved good-bye to the women and started the car. "She's not my worry," he muttered to himself, "but it could be interesting working with her." He scowled. "Still wish Jenny had come, too. She's been around here long enough to know about the cruise industry. And we had some good times in high school." *Kind of wanted to know what she was like after six years,* he admitted silently. *Guess I'll never know.*

Ryan stopped by Sea-Land Grocery to pick up some chocolate milk and a frozen dinner. *Still light,* he thought, getting back in the car. *I could work on the boat for a while tonight.*

two

Laurette stood in the midst of the Victorian decor thinking the place must have been copied from a page in a magazine. There were marble-top tables, fringed lamps, and lacy doilies everywhere. She listened politely to Edith, who seemed to want to explain where everything had come from. Finally she broke into her hostess's monologue. "Excuse me. I'm sorry. I'd like to freshen up. Would you mind?"

"Why, of course not, dear. How thoughtless of me. We can chat later when you've had a chance to settle in."

Edith closed the door to Laurette's room, still cheerfully talking, apparently to herself, her voice fading as she walked away.

"Hope I can find a permanent home soon," she muttered, pulling open her backpack. Her stomach grumbled, indicating the bag of peanuts she had eaten on the plane had long since disappeared. "As soon as I've washed up, I'll walk back into town and find a place to eat."

She spent a few minutes unpacking and had just started for her jacket when she heard a knock at the door.

"I have some tea made. Wouldn't you like a cup, dear?" Edith offered when Laurette opened it. The woman had tightly permed white hair and wore a large apron over her ample figure.

Seeing the pleading look in the woman's eyes, Laurette nodded and set her jacket down. She followed her hostess into the kitchen, where her eyes were accosted by bright yellow walls and flowered curtains. She started to the chair Edith indicated but stopped when she heard a ghastly noise. Had someone screamed?

13

"Oh, Lucy, be still. This nice young lady will be with us a few days."

Laurette looked at the large Siamese cat wrapping itself around her legs and reached down to scratch between its dark ears. A plate of muffins sat next to the teapot on the table, and Laurette's stomach began to growl loudly. She sat down and took the cup Edith offered her.

"I don't get many roomers this time of year. It's nice to have someone in the house."

"Thank you. I'll be here until I can find a permanent place to rent, if that's all right."

"Of course, dear. Will you be working with Ryan Nichols?" Edith passed her the plate of muffins.

"I have a summer job with Southeast Alaska Maritime, so it seems I will for a little while." Laurette chose a large berry muffin and took a bite.

"He's such a nice boy. He was just a child when his father died. His mother fell to pieces, and young Ryan took care of her."

Laurette nearly choked. Quickly she sipped some tea, wishing she knew how to stop this conversation. She took another bite of muffin.

"Stayed right with her until she up and ran off with a musician."

Laurette put down her cup to ask about the town's history, hoping to divert the woman, but her hostess didn't even stop for breath.

As she reached to refill her guest's cup, Edith continued. "She did teach Ryan well. My friend Molly and I go to dinner at the Dockside Hotel once a month. We always make sure Ryan will be playing the night we go."

"Playing?" Laurette managed to sputter.

"Why, yes. He plays jazz piano in the lounge. We just love to listen to him. His mother taught music, you know."

Laurette took another of the muffins Edith passed her to stave off starvation. "Thank you. These are very good. Did you make—"

"Isabel Nichols used to play the organ at our church. Ryan always came with her." She paused for a second and cocked her head to one side. "He quit coming when his mother no longer played for us." She took a sip of tea.

Laurette had wolfed down the second muffin and pushed back from the table. "Thank you for the refreshments, Edith. Will you excuse me? I'm really very tired. It's been a long day. I think I'll turn in now."

"Of course, dear. Good night."

❧

The clock read 6:05. "I'd better get up and get moving. Don't know how long it will take to walk to the office." She started to sit up and gasped when she felt something warm on the bed next to her. Lucy looked up and yawned. Laurette scratched her ears, and the cat went back to sleep.

Ten minutes later, Laurette stepped out of the shower, dried off, then wrapped her hair in the towel. She picked up the jeans and light blue sweater she had unpacked last night. As she dressed, her stomach complained that two small muffins had been a poor substitute for a good supper. She stepped out of the bathroom and smelled coffee brewing, instantly hoping Edith wouldn't say any more about Ryan's private life over breakfast. Laurette abhorred gossip.

Soon Laurette was polishing off her third blueberry pancake when Edith offered her more coffee. "No thanks. Everything has been delicious, but I need to get to work. I'll let you know as soon as I find a place to live. Mr. Healy said he would help me."

"He and his wife are fine people. You can trust them to find you a good home."

Makes me sound like a stray cat, she thought wryly as she got up from the table. "Thank you again for breakfast."

"I have a bridge game tonight, so I may not be here when you come home. The door will be open."

"Okay. Have a nice time. I'll see you in the morning."

❧

Laurette arrived at the office fifteen minutes early. Tyler stood at the fax machine reading messages. "Good morning. Did you rest well?"

"My landlady is a bit talkative, but I did get to bed fairly early."

Tyler's laugh rang through the room. "Edith does get lonesome. Diane said I should have brought you home and saved you the lodging expense. She's working on finding you a place to live." He turned and answered the phone on his desk.

Laurette looked out the window while he handled the call. A beautiful white cruise ship floated on the still water outside the marina.

"You can handle this one," Tyler told her, hanging up the phone. "There's luggage at the airport that didn't make it to the ship." He picked up a set of keys and a slip of paper. "The van's parked right over there." He pointed to the parking lot where she'd been the day before. "Can you find your way to the airport?"

She nodded. "How did the luggage end up at the airport instead of on the ship?"

He shook his head. "Happens all the time. Passengers don't read their instructions and don't have their bags where they should be. In this case the passengers flew into Seattle early. They left their bags in their hotel room with the cruise line tags on them and expected someone to pick them up." He smiled. "Sometimes it's the airlines who foul up, and the cruise lines aren't perfect, either. They're handling thousands of pieces of luggage, and it doesn't always work the way it should. That's why we're here."

"I'm on my way." Laurette grabbed the keys and glanced at the details he'd hastily written down for her.

"Come back here with the luggage, then either Ryan or I will take the bags out to the ship."

When she returned, Ryan waved at her, holding the phone to his ear in the other hand. He ended the conversation and told her, "Let's go. I'll take you out to the ship. There's a tender due in ten minutes."

Laurette tried to lengthen her stride to keep up with his long legs. He grabbed the two suitcases out of the van, and they rushed down the ramp to the dock. People were waiting to get on what looked like a tour boat.

"Every ship has its own tenders. In Sitka, we don't have a dock where the large ships can tie up, so they use these boats to ferry passengers back and forth." Ryan moved toward the skipper. "Hi, Don. How ya doing?"

"Who's your girlfriend?" the crew member asked as they boarded the tender.

"Like you to meet Laurette. She'll be working for SAM this summer."

Laurette nodded to the man who seemed busy moving the boat away from the dock and back toward the cruise ship. She stood quietly while he and Ryan talked about fishing.

Once aboard the ship, after the luggage was delivered to the steward, Ryan asked, "Would you like a tour?"

The ship's opulence was overwhelming. "This thing is huge. I'll need to drop bread crumbs to find my way out if I ever have to come aboard alone. Are they all this big?"

Ryan grinned. "Some are bigger, but you'll learn your way around in no time." He led her through salons and restaurants all the way to the top deck.

"I'm impressed," Laurette said.

"Think you'd like to live like this?"

"Not me. I'm just a country girl," she protested.

"I like your attitude."

Laurette liked his smile. She followed him back down to catch the next tender going ashore.

She felt comfortable with Ryan today. Maybe some of the things Edith had said about him had made her more sympathetic. *It did help to have him being friendly,* she admitted, glancing at his long, slender fingers. What would it be like to hear him play the piano?

Back at the office, Tyler caught Laurette's attention. "My wife called and wants you to talk to John Stevenson. A friend at our church told her he's looking for someone to stay at his mother's house. Says she's getting a bit senile, and he'd like to have someone there at night and checking on her while he's out fishing."

Laurette welcomed the chance—until she saw the look on Ryan's face. *Just how senile is this woman?*

❧

Ryan tried to hide his feelings. *Should I warn Laurette?* He looked at his boss. What were he and Diane thinking, sending Laurette out there? He sighed and poured a cup of coffee.

Silently sipping his coffee, he watched Laurette. *She bubbles,* he thought, smiling inwardly.

The usual details of taking care of ships and passengers filled the day. When it was almost time to go home, Tyler looked up from a stack of new faxes. "Ryan, could you drop Laurette by John Stevenson's boat on your way home? He's at the Alaskan Native Brotherhood Marina. I'm sure he'll see that she gets back to Edith's."

Impulsively, Ryan asked her, "Want to get something to eat before we go see John?"

"I'd like that."

Moments later, they settled into a booth in a small café. "They have great fish-and-chips," he told Laurette as a waitress walked up.

"Drinking the usual, Ryan?"

He nodded. "And an order of fish-and-chips." Pointing at his seatmate, he said, "This is Laurette, Connie. She's working for Southeast this summer."

"Welcome to Sitka. You addicted to chocolate milk, too?"

"I'd like a cola with my fish-and-chips, please."

Ryan watched as Laurette sipped her water. Her warm brown eyes seemed to sparkle. She had a smattering of freckles across her nose. The damp air left her chestnut hair in tight ringlets around her heart-shaped face. *She brings sunshine to everything she touches,* he thought.

While they waited for their meals, she asked, "Does this John Stevenson live on his boat?"

"No, he's got a place in town. He must be getting ready for the halibut opening."

Laurette put her water glass down. "What's a halibut opening? Sounds like a Broadway play."

"John's a commercial fisherman. The Fisheries Department sets certain hours when the commercial boats can go out."

"I don't know about taking care of his mother," she said, abruptly changing the subject. "I looked at the schedule in the office, and I don't think I'll be around much, what with more and more ships coming in after this week."

Ryan welcomed the waitress with their meals. He still didn't think he should get involved. *She can make her own choice on this one,* he thought, grabbing a piece of fish.

"I'd like to find a place to live as soon as I can."

"I see Edith when I play at the Dockside Hotel, but I don't know her at all." He gulped some of his chocolate milk.

"She told me you played piano in the lounge there." She took a bite of fish. "You're right. This is good."

"The job with SAM is seasonal. I pick up some tips playing piano in the winter months." He grinned. "It pays for my drinking habit."

They ate in comfortable silence. Soon they'd polished off the last of their fish-and-chips, and Ryan wiped his hands on a napkin. "Ready to go?"

"Uh-huh." She drank down the last of her soda and reached for the check. "I want to pay for my own," Laurette said firmly.

"You leave the tip." He smiled and snatched the check from her.

❧

"Rain get to you?" he asked as they walked back to the car in a fine mist.

"I spent four years at the University of Washington in Seattle. Got used to the rain. Did you go south for college?"

"No—stayed here and went to Sheldon Jackson."

He kept his thoughts to himself while he turned onto Katlian Street and slowed to look at the boats. "Most people call this the ANB Harbor. I'm not sure what slip John's in. We'd better park and walk."

"They all look alike to me," Laurette said, staring up at the tall rigging on the boats tied up along the dock. "Do you know Mr. Stevenson well?"

"My dad fished with him years ago." Ryan waved to a man coiling rope on the bow of a boat. "Hey, John," he called.

Laurette followed Ryan to where the fisherman stepped onto the dock. "John, this is Laurette, the woman Diane Healy called about," Ryan explained.

Laurette stepped next to Ryan and shook John's hand. "Nice to know you, Laurette."

"Thank y—"

"When's the opening?" Ryan asked him, realizing too late he'd interrupted her. He gave her a look he hoped showed an apology.

"We get forty-eight hours starting at six in the morning."

"You fish for forty-eight hours?" Laurette's voice held disbelief.

John smiled at her. "That's how I make a living." He turned to Ryan. "Thanks for bringing her by. I can see that she gets back to where she's staying."

Ryan looked at Laurette. She seemed okay with the plan, so he bade them good-bye and walked back to his car.

He brooded over her remark that she had gone to the U of W. He had worked hard to get the grades to enroll there. He kicked a rock on the path. "Stayed to take care of Mother," he whispered bitterly.

Why do you stay here? Your mother's gone. Nothing to hold you in Sitka now, his conscience taunted him.

He breathed deeply, drawing the fresh salt air into his lungs. Somewhere on the hill rising above the harbor, an eagle called.

Did you only stay for her, or was it because you couldn't bear to leave Sitka?

Ryan shook off the thoughts and the drops falling around him, then got in his car and drove back to his trailer.

three

Laurette watched Ryan walk up the dock before turning to John Stevenson. He appeared to be in his early fifties. Wisps of gray hair peeked from under his seaman's cap. He stood three or four inches taller than she did.

"Come inside out of the rain." He offered to help her step onto the bow of the boat.

She followed his stocky, jean-clad figure through the door into a neat-looking galley. He motioned for her to take a seat on a bench behind the table.

"Coffee?" he asked, reaching for mugs hanging above the stove.

She nodded, noting the brackets around the stove burners; she guessed they held pots and pans in place so they wouldn't slide off if the boat rocked. Cooking on a boat would be a whole new experience.

John set a mug in front of her and took a seat across the table. His smile crinkled his weather-beaten face. "Now let's get to know each other. Diane Healy told me you needed a room to rent this summer."

"That's right. I'll be here until the middle of October. After that I don't have plans."

"Well, my mother is getting on in years. She's been getting more and more forgetful. When a friend called to tell me she had gone to pick Mother up for church, and Mom didn't remember it was Sunday, I started getting worried."

"I wouldn't be around very much. And I really wouldn't be able to take care of her, since I'm working for SAM," Laurette said quickly.

He nodded. "I know all about Southeast Maritime." He sipped his coffee. "Mother is very independent. She doesn't need a nurse." John chuckled softly. "As a matter of fact, I've had to be carefully diplomatic to get her approval to rent a room." He put the cup down. "I take care of Mom because I want to, but she doesn't like to take money from me." His dark eyes sparkled with mischief. "I suggested that if she rented her spare room, she would have a little more spending money. I know she'll want you to share the whole house—feel free to cook, wash clothes, or do whatever you want. Having you come in and out each day will give her something to look forward to. And it will make me feel better knowing someone is there to check on her each evening."

"It sounds good to me. I'm staying at a B and B right now, but I couldn't afford that for very long." Laurette sipped the coffee.

"Mother and I decided on a rent of two hundred a month."

Laurette gasped. "I pay fifty dollars a night now. Is there a catch I don't know about?" She put the mug down with a thump.

John's good-natured laugh eased her mind. "I would be willing to pay *you* to stay there. This way we both win. You get a cheaper rent and Mom gets a companion. Would you like to meet my mother before you decide?"

"I think that would be wise—for both of us," Laurette said emphatically.

John picked up the cups and put them in the sink. "We can run over there now if you'd like."

"Aren't you busy getting ready for the opening tomorrow?"

"I'm as ready as I'll ever be. Just down here fussing with the boat this evening. I planned to see Mother again before I left, anyway." He opened the door for her. "This way you can go with me."

She climbed into his pickup truck. He pulled onto Katlian Street for a few blocks before turning down a small road leading up the hill overlooking what John called Thompson Harbor. At the top she spotted a neat-looking frame house with a wraparound deck. There were flowerpots on the deck with daffodils in bloom.

"Mom loves her flowers. She can get things to grow where no one else is successful. She'll be setting out geraniums as soon as the daffodils are spent."

Laurette followed him into the entryway, which appeared to be a place to hang coats and stash boots. Beyond the mudroom, she spotted a laundry with cupboards built along the opposite wall. John opened a door into the kitchen. It wasn't new, but it appeared serviceable to Laurette. The room looked bright and clean. When they entered the large living room, a spry elderly woman got up and gave John a big hug.

"Mother, I've brought a young lady to meet you." He kept one arm around his mother's shoulders as he turned to introduce Laurette.

"Oh, how pretty you are." A smile lit the woman's wrinkled face.

Laurette offered her hand.

"Mother, this is Laurette Martel. Laurette, this is my mother, Ruth Stevenson."

"And you have a pretty name," Ruth said, taking Laurette's hand in both of hers.

Her sincere welcome warmed Laurette. Ruth's steel-gray hair had been pulled back into a bun at the nape of her neck, and her clothes were clean and tidy. "I'm glad to meet you," Laurette said politely.

"Come sit down." Ruth motioned toward the other lounge chair and then to the davenport against the opposite wall. It stood between two doors Laurette thought must go to the bedrooms. Looking at the end of the room, she saw the view from a large window. She walked to the built-in window seat. "It's beautiful. You can see the water and the far islands."

Ruth came up behind her. "My Warren cut the tall trees when we built here. Now it's just scrub that won't block the view but does give us privacy."

"You have a lovely home." Laurette took a seat on the davenport across from the lounge chairs. John muted the television his mother had been watching.

"Have you brought this girl to rent the room?" Ruth asked her son.

"Don't you think you should get to know her better before you invite her to live with you?" he asked his mother with a wink at Laurette. "I think you're just eager to start getting rent money to spend."

Ruth giggled like a young girl. "Just a little mad money, Son. I won't go wild or anything." She turned to Laurette. "Are you new to Sitka?"

"Yes. I'll be working for Southeast Alaska Maritime this summer, and I do need a place to live."

"Well, let me show you the room, and if you would like to try it for a week to see if you can put up with an old lady like me, that would be fine with me."

Laurette liked Ruth, but she welcomed the chance to try the situation before making a serious commitment.

"And you can check me out to see if I make too much noise," Laurette said, looking at the bed, dresser, and nightstand in the front bedroom.

"Oh, you don't like that horrid music, do you?" Ruth asked in alarm.

It was Laurette's turn to laugh. "No, I never got into hard rock. I do have some tapes and CDs, but they're prayer and praise songs."

"That would be nice. Do you have a church?"

"The Healys have invited me to go with them." The women

had returned to their seats in the living room.

"Well, I go to St. Peter's-by-the-Sea. It's one thing around here that's older than I am."

The more Laurette listened to this upbeat, personable woman, the more she liked her. Spending time with Ruth could be like having her own special grandmother. They chatted for a few more minutes, then Laurette announced, "I can move in as soon as I can find a vehicle. This would be too far for me to walk to work."

"Maybe I could help," John offered. "My cousin has a mini pickup he said he wanted to sell. Would you like me to call about it?"

"Yes, thank you." Laurette watched as he pulled a cell phone out of his pocket and walked into the kitchen.

"I can't get used to all this newfangled stuff. A phone that isn't plugged in," Ruth sputtered. "Now tell me about your home."

Laurette answered Ruth's questions about the farm and her parents until John returned.

"Mike says Emmy has gone to a Bible study meeting, and he's home alone. He'd welcome company." John then said to Laurette, "Says he still has his small pickup for sale. He claims it runs good. Would you like to check it out?"

Laurette looked at her watch. "If you can tell me where it is, I'll ask Ryan to take me there tomorrow."

"I can take you right now if you'd like. It isn't that late. Have you had supper?"

"Yes, we ate before we came to see you. But it's getting late, and you have to be on the water early."

"That's no problem. Let's go see Mike." He pulled his mother up to give her a big hug. "I'm going halibut fishing in the morning. I'll call you as soon as I'm close enough in to get a signal on the cell phone."

"You be careful." She turned to Laurette. "Do you have

my phone number? Then you can let me know when you'll move in."

Impulsively, Laurette gave Ruth a quick hug. It felt good to put her cheek against the papery thin one of her new friend. "I'll call you tomorrow."

❧

"Mike has a tugboat out at Jamestown Bay," John told her as he drove back through town and took Sawmill Creek Road.

"Your mother is delightful."

He smiled. "It's sad to have her mind start to fade. She's always been so sharp. After my dad died, I worried about her, but she's done fine on her own for twenty years."

He pulled into a small road toward the ever-present water. "Mike and Emmy have a house in town, but they stay on the boat most of the time. He does a lot of work for SAM, so you'll run into him this summer." They passed a metal building. "When he isn't on the tug, he's in that shop puttering on something."

A big man in overalls and a plaid shirt greeted them at the dock. "I was just coming to get the truck out for you. Come on in the shed. That way you can see it without getting wet." He motioned to the mist filling the air.

Laurette followed the men. When Mike flipped on the light, she took a second look at the faded little truck. It had rust on the fenders, and a sheet of plywood covered the truck bed. She wondered how much rust that covered up.

"Not much to look at," Mike admitted. "A crewman of mine was moving south and needed money, so I bought it. Been working on it this past winter. Runs real good. Want to try it?"

Might as well look, Laurette thought, opening the driver's door. "It only has fifty thousand miles on it. How old is it?" she asked in wonder when she started the motor.

"Ten years old, but it's only fourteen miles from one end

of Sitka to the other. Don't put on many miles around here."
Mike chuckled. "Take it out for a spin."

Laurette backed out of the shed and drove up the driveway
and down the road to a place to turn around.

"It handles great," she said when she returned. "Motor sounds
smooth. How much do you want for it?" she asked Mike.

Mike named a price before asking, "What's a pretty little
thing like you know about motors?"

"I grew up on a wheat farm and learned to drive a tractor
when I was twelve. My dad said if I wanted to run the
equipment, I had to learn how to take care of it. He taught
me some mechanics." She smiled. "My kid brother, Brian,
didn't learn the mechanics, but he's a whiz at running the
farm. Dad said he got his son and daughter mixed up."

"Now you don't have to do any grease monkey work. If that
truck gives you any problems, you bring it back to me and I'll
have it purring in no time," Mike told her.

"He would, too," John assured her.

Laurette thought of her bank balance. Her dad had told her
to buy a clunker that she could sell cheap when she left Sitka.
Wait 'til I send him a picture of this, she thought, laughing to
herself. "Will you take my check? It's on a Seattle bank."

"Where are you going to go around this town? Only way
you can get out is by boat or by plane, and I doubt the truck
is that important."

Laurette pulled her checkbook out of her pocket. "May I
borrow a pen?"

Mike led her to his workbench. She marveled at how each
tool had been cleaned and put back in place.

With the paperwork completed, John asked, "Can you find
your way home?"

"Like Mike says, I can't go far, so how can I get lost?" She
laughed with the men.

She shook hands with the cousins. "I'll call your mother

tomorrow, John. I should be able to move in with her right away."

He patted her hand. "I'll sleep a lot better knowing you're with her. God bless you," he said and released her hand. She waved to the men and drove her new vehicle back to town.

❧

Ryan pulled into the parking lot early the next morning. He parked in his usual spot but stopped when he got out. "Now who owns that piece of junk?" he muttered.

"You like my new truck?"

"That's yours?" *What will this girl do next?* he wondered, shaking his head at Laurette. "It's a rusted-out wreck. How will you keep it running?" He looked at her and wondered who had sold her this disaster on wheels.

"I can keep it running."

"You?" He shook his head. *She's certifiable. And I've got to spend the summer with her.*

"I've been working on farm machines since I could see over the hood. I can keep it going."

"Farm machinery!" he exclaimed. "You expect me to believe that?"

"Ryan, I grew up on a big wheat farm in eastern Washington. Machinery is crucial to our way of life, and I learned how to take care of it. My dad didn't treat me like some weak little girl. He taught me to work the fields and the equipment we used."

He just stood there, dumbfounded.

"Sorry, but I've got to get postage stamps," she said with a smile, pointing her thumb over her shoulder toward a ship. "Mustn't keep the customer waiting. See you later."

Motor sounds good, he thought as she pulled out of the parking lot. *Wonder how she found a vehicle so fast.* He started to the office, pleased that she was picking up the job so quickly. "Things might work out okay," he muttered to himself, walking up the stairs to the Southeast Alaska Maritime office.

four

Laurette stopped by a hardware store before going to the post office. She had to buy a tarp. In Sitka, blue sky or not, it could be raining five minutes from now. She moved her things from the truck's tiny cab, where she'd hardly been able to see over them, into the cargo bed and tucked the tarp securely around her duffel bag and box.

As she climbed back into the driver's seat, she remembered the scene at breakfast. Laurette hadn't unpacked many of her belongings, so it hadn't taken her long to stuff everything back in her duffel bag and backpack. Edith had been busy whipping up an omelet when she went into the kitchen.

"Did you enjoy your card game?" Laurette asked, sitting down with a cup of coffee.

Edith started describing every hand, allowing Laurette time to enjoy her toast, jam, and omelet before breaking into her landlady's monologue.

"I've rented a room, Edith. I'll get my things out of your bedroom this morning. Thank you for your hospitality. I'm sure we'll meet around town while I'm here this summer." Laurette picked up her coffee cup and did not look at Edith for fear she'd see that lonely look in her eyes again.

Edith gushed with good cheer and tried to pry loose the name of the place where Laurette planned to move.

"The Healys found someone wanting to rent a room. It looks like I'll be working long hours and won't be there very much. I think it'll be fine." Laurette put her cup down and pulled out her checkbook. "Let me pay you for my time here." She smiled. "I'll miss your good cooking."

Edith kept dithering but took the offered money and wished Laurette good luck. Lucy came by to rub her legs, purring loudly, as if adding a feline farewell.

"Now that I'm checked out," Laurette muttered as she entered the post office, "I sure hope the room with Ruth works out."

Back at the SAM office, she read through the fax messages. "I can't believe all the things they need to keep the ships going."

"We're talking thousands of people. A huge business, and it's a floating one. Can't just run down to the corner to pick up a loaf of bread," Tyler told her. "What have we got there?" he asked, pointing to the messages.

"The ships coming in today want everything from prescriptions filled for passengers to finding lost luggage." She sifted through the stack. "These are from ships due later in the week. They're ordering fresh flowers and produce. How do we do that?"

Tyler reached for the page and scanned it before answering. "I'll call Seattle and have it flown in. I need you to go to the bank and get some change. The steward on the ship due in at two o'clock wants us to deliver it when they anchor today." Tyler reached into his desk and withdrew a ledger. "I'm going to give you a check; they need the funds in those denominations," he said, pointing at the page on his desk. He wrote out the check, then handed it and the fax to her. "By the way, Diane wants to know how you made out with John Stevenson."

"His mother is very sweet. I'm going to move in for a week or so and make sure we both like the arrangement. John took me by his cousin Mike's and I bought a little truck from him."

"We do a lot of business with Mike Littlefield. He takes the harbor pilots out to the ships for us, and I call on him when we have freight that needs moving. Good man. If he sold you a vehicle, it's in great running order." Tyler smiled. "Mike's a fantastic mechanic. Keeps his old tug in tip-top condition."

"The truck doesn't look like much, but it'll serve me for the summer."

"You plan on moving right away?"

"I've called Ruth Stevenson and arranged to take my stuff up there after work."

The phone rang, ending their conversation. Laurette headed for the bank.

❧

Stopping by the fish-and-chips place, Laurette picked up take-out orders for her and Ruth. "Have you eaten yet?" she called as she entered the kitchen.

Ruth came to the door looking puzzled. "Is it lunchtime?"

Laurette didn't correct her. Instead, she took plates from the cupboard and put a kettle on to boil for tea. "Come sit down. We'll eat while things are hot. I'll bring my things in later."

"I didn't expect you to cook for me," Ruth protested. "I'll make dinner tomorrow night."

Laurette poured hot water into the teapot. "That would be nice." She sat down and asked, "Would you like to say grace?"

Ruth rewarded her with a big smile. "You're a believer." She patted Laurette's hand. "I'm glad."

After devouring the fish-and-chips, the women sat over cups of tea while Ruth talked about her sister. "Esther was a year older than me. We grew up in an orphanage in Rose, Alaska. It's in the interior." She smiled and sipped her tea. "That's why when we came here we went to St. Peter's Church. The Episcopal Church ran the orphanage, and we grew up with the liturgy." She shrugged. "I like knowing the service will follow the same pattern each week. I get confused easily these days, and it helps to have things I can depend on."

"Let me wash the dishes. Why don't you go sit in your chair and I'll be there shortly."

Laurette carried her bags and boxes to her bedroom. When she unpacked her laptop computer, she decided to e-mail her parents. She typed a quick note and went to the living room to plug the modem into a phone jack so she could send her message.

"Is that one of those computer things?" Ruth asked.

Laurette nodded as she shut the machine down.

"My granddaughter Marty is one of those computer people. She says she's a nerd, whatever that is."

"Does she live around here?"

"Oh, no. She works in Seattle. I think she's married to that computer. Nearly thirty and not even a boyfriend. I don't think I'm ever going to have great-grandchildren. John's boy is no better. Craig's in the Coast Guard." She picked up the book in her lap. "Marty sent me this. Said I could read the big print."

Laurette looked at the red leather Bible. "Does the large print help?"

Ruth scowled. "Yes, but I still like the King James better. Just an old-fashioned old woman, I guess."

Laurette jumped up. "Let me get my King James and I'll read to you."

"Bless you, dear."

❧

The evening passed quickly. When Ruth's head started to nod, Laurette put the Bible down. "I need to be up early. Time I got some sleep. Good night." She kissed Ruth on the cheek and went to her room.

Laurette glanced at her watch and muttered, "Too late to unpack. I'll pull out enough for tomorrow and get settled later."

The house was silent when the alarm went off. Laurette showered and dressed as quietly as she could. Finding cereal, she poured herself a bowl and made a note to check the cupboards. "I don't know whether Ruth eats regularly, so I'll start doing some cooking," she whispered to herself.

The pattern of her days didn't vary. Only the tasks to be done to help keep the cruise ships working smoothly changed. She learned to keep her day pack with her. When she took a passenger to the medical clinic, she could read while she waited for them to see the doctor. Tyler explained that there were doctors aboard the ships, but insurance coverage made it necessary for some passengers to seek medical care while in port.

On Sunday, Tyler suggested Laurette take time off to attend church. "Diane will meet you in the parking lot. That way you'll have someone to sit with."

"I wouldn't recognize your wife, but I'll recognize Kate and David from the pictures on your desk," Laurette quipped. "Your children are adorable."

Tyler beamed with pride even when he protested the four-year-old girl and six-year-old boy were both imps and always into mischief.

Ryan had been filling his coffee cup during this conversation. Laurette took her own cup over to be topped off and asked, "Do you go to the same church, Ryan?"

"Not much for church anymore. My mother used to play the organ at church, but I haven't gone back since she left. I'll be around here to take care of business." He sipped his coffee and headed for an incoming fax.

❧

Laurette had disappeared when he returned from picking up luggage at the airport. Tyler had gone aboard a ship with immigration papers. Ryan knew his boss did that so the immigration officer could have time off. He picked up the local paper and opened the carton of chocolate milk he had purchased on his way back to the office.

"I wonder if Laurette likes music," he mused. "The annual music festival will be here in a couple weeks." The phone rang, and he put down the paper.

Later that day, Laurette greeted his invitation with the cheerful enthusiasm she seemed to have for everything. "What kind of music will this be?"

"The emphasis is on chamber music. It's an annual thing with professionals coming in from around the country. I've got tickets for Tuesday night at Centennial Hall." Her smile warmed him. *I'm glad I asked her,* he thought.

"Sounds like a wonderful evening. Do I have to get dressed up?"

He chuckled. "In Sitka, dressing up means a clean pair of jeans."

"Will you come have supper with Ruth and me before the concert?"

Ryan didn't know how to answer. "Do you cook for Ruth?"

Laurette gave him her hundred-watt smile. "She forgets to eat sometimes, so I try to cook up something in the evening. That way I know she eats at least once a day."

"If it's good enough for Ruth, it's good enough for me. What time should I be there?"

&

Delicious smells greeted Ryan when he entered Ruth's house at the appointed time.

Ruth welcomed him warmly. "I used to know your mother. She played at our church sometimes. Is she well?"

"I hear from her occasionally. She and her husband live in Chicago, and as far as I know, both are well and enjoying music."

"And do you play?" she asked, letting him seat her at the table.

"A little."

"He plays jazz piano at the Dockside Hotel," Laurette said as she put a Crock-Pot in the middle of the table. "Shall we eat while this is hot?"

Ryan kept his head down while Laurette said grace. He did sneak a peek at her face and found her eyes closed and her expression peaceful. *She's a gentle person,* he thought, taking the bowl she offered him after the prayer.

"Have some bread," Ruth urged, passing the hot French bread. "I didn't know I got a cook as well as a housemate. She even reads to me. What do you think of that?"

Ryan swallowed the bite of bread. "I do think you got yourself a good cook in the bargain. This stew is tasty." He grinned at Laurette. "And she even has my favorite drink." He held up his glass of chocolate milk in a toast to the ladies.

Ryan watched the two women and saw the bond between them. He picked up the bowls and carried them to the sink for Laurette. "I'll dry," he offered. *Is it her faith that makes her so sweet?*

ప

Later, as they entered the auditorium, Laurette gasped.

"It's awesome. I've never seen anything like this."

She's looking at the windows, he realized. *I've seen them for years and never thought they were special.* "When the weather is clear, the curtains at the back of the stage are left open." The view had her eyes shining, and he looked at it, trying to see it as she was, for the first time. The forested green hills were topped with snow. "You're right," he admitted. "It's awesome."

Ryan spent most of the concert watching Laurette. Her pleasure in the music made her face glow. He wanted to take her hand and share her joy, but he feared it would offend her. The music brought memories flooding back. He missed playing the classics. Jazz was better than nothing, and the piano at the hotel was the only piano he had access to. She looked concerned when he sighed. The piece ended, and as they applauded, he asked, "Do you like it?"

"Oh, yes. The acoustics are very good." She smiled up at him. "And so are the musicians."

When they walked back to his car, she asked, "Do you play classics or just jazz?"

"I prefer the classics, but I don't have room for a piano at home. Started playing at the Dockside Hotel just to get to a piano occasionally."

"You said your mother and her husband were musicians. Did she play at the festival?"

Ryan groaned inwardly and started the car. "One year they needed a pianist, so she filled in. That's when she met Harvey. He plays first violin for the Chicago Symphony."

"You must be very proud."

"Bitter is more like it. When the pulp mill closed, my dad started fishing to make a living. He was lost at sea four years later."

"I'm sorry. How old were you?" He could hear the concern in her voice.

"Sixteen." Lulled by the music and Laurette's genuine caring, he continued. "I dreamed of going to college down south, but Mother begged me not to leave her. She couldn't get over losing my dad." He glanced at Laurette. Her eyes shone with deep compassion. "I stayed with Mom and got my bachelor's degree in business at the local college."

"How long has your mother been married?" Her soft voice soothed him.

"About four years. I was twenty when she met Harvey. She married him six months later and moved to Chicago." He shrugged. "I just stayed here, finished college, and kept working for SAM." He parked in the driveway at Ruth's.

"You've let the bitterness rob you. Why?"

Puzzled, he looked at her. "I don't know."

"Do you blame God for making your life miserable?"

He cringed inwardly but answered honestly. "I don't know what God has to do with it. My dad's gone. Mom left me behind. I've just stumbled along on my own for so long, it seems trusting Him didn't help me much. I don't know that I blame Him, but I sure do feel—empty, sometimes."

"You don't have to be alone. God didn't cause your sorrow, but He's there to help you cope with it." She laid her hand on his arm. "I won't preach, but you might give some thought to letting Jesus bear your burden."

Coming from this sweet woman, the words didn't cause him to bristle like they had when others said them. "I'll keep your suggestion in mind."

"Thank you for a wonderful evening. I did enjoy the music and hope someday to hear you play. Now I'd better get some sleep, or I won't hear the alarm in the morning."

She popped out of the car before he could open the door. Ryan watched her bounce up the steps where she turned to wave before going in the house.

"She is some kind of special," he told the night as he started the drive back home.

five

A week after the festival, Sitka was enveloped in fog. Passengers from the three ships in port were cranky and demanding. They complained to the steward and cruise director who in turn expected Southeast Alaska Maritime to fix all their problems. Luggage that should have arrived by airfreight went on to Juneau. Laurette felt pulled in six different directions.

Coming back to the office after taking a passenger to the medical clinic, she soon found Ryan with a fresh pot of coffee.

"How you holding up?" he asked.

She took the proffered cup and sank into a chair. "I'm thankful for rain gear."

"You heard about the little kid selling newspapers to the passengers?"

"No." She sipped her coffee.

"One tourist asked him if it ever stopped raining in Sitka. The boy told him he didn't know. He was only eight years old."

Laurette giggled. "You made that up."

"Standard joke. Use it every time the clouds move in." He drank from his mug. "You're my latest victim of poor humor."

She shook her head. *Is it me, or is Ryan acting more cheerful? He's kind of fun to be around.*

The phone rang, and the new office clerk, Debbie, yelled for one of them to take a call. There were two new helpers in the office. They had both worked for SAM before and helped take over some of the office duties. Laurette accepted the task of getting medicine for a passenger. It meant collecting the original prescription information details, coordinating with the pharmacy in Sitka, then delivering it to the ship.

At the end of the day, Laurette dragged herself to her little truck and drove home. "Maybe we'll have soup for supper. I'm too tired to shop," she muttered as she pulled into the driveway.

The television was on, but Ruth didn't come to the kitchen. Laurette found her sitting in her chair, dressed in her housedress with her nightgown pulled over it.

"Oh, I've been waiting for you to get up. What will we have for breakfast?" Ruth asked innocently.

Laurette closed her eyes and said a quick prayer. *Guide me, Jesus. I love this dear woman, and I want to help her.* "You enjoy your TV show. I'll fix us something," she told Ruth.

"Soup for breakfast won't do," she murmured as she opened the refrigerator. She took eggs and cheese to the counter and lifted the toaster down from the cupboard.

After enjoying her cheese omelet and toast, Ruth wandered back to the living room. Laurette cleaned up the kitchen and joined her housemate.

"Why don't I run you a hot bath with bubbles," she suggested to Ruth.

"I think that would feel good," Ruth agreed.

Laurette managed to help Ruth out of the layers of clothes she wore and into the tub. Sure that she was safely settled, Laurette left her to bathe. She knocked on the bathroom door a few minutes later.

"Come in."

"I've got your nightgown right here," she said. Ruth grabbed the safety bar and stood when Laurette held up a large bath towel. *Kind of like caring for a child,* Laurette thought tenderly. She led Ruth to her bed and tucked her under the covers. "I'll get my Bible and read to you for a little while if you like."

"Bless you, dear."

She had no idea how long she sat at Ruth's bedside.

Finally, Ruth's eyes started to droop. "I'll read one more." Knowing it was Ruth's favorite, she read Psalm 98 before gently kissing her friend's cheek and turning out the light.

Laurette tossed a load of clothes into the washer and finally managed to crawl into bed. It seemed as though she had just fallen asleep when her cell phone rang.

Tyler sounded frantic. "I'm sorry to call you, but I can't get ahold of Ryan. We have a heart attack victim on the ship due in at four this morning. I have to be on the early flight to Ketchikan. Can you be at the dock with an ambulance when the ship anchors?"

"Will they bring the patient to shore on a tender?"

"Yes. They have stabilized the man, but we need to accompany him into the hospital."

"I'll take care of it." Laurette checked her clock after Tyler had given her the pertinent details. She had less than an hour to get organized. Shaking off her fatigue, she called the hospital to advise them what had happened. The emergency room would be standing by, and they would dispatch an ambulance to the dock.

Pulling on jeans and a warm sweater, Laurette grabbed her day pack and ran for her truck. She parked her rig at the SAM office, then got a company van pulled close to where the ambulance would park. The medics arrived moments after she did.

Fingers of light pushed over the horizon while she stood with the medical technicians. Together they watched the lights of the huge ship as it set anchor in the harbor. As soon as the medics saw the tender head to shore, they wheeled a gurney to the dock.

Laurette stood back while the tender's crew carried the patient, still strapped to a crash board, up the dock and placed him on the waiting gurney. She went to the distraught woman stepping off the tender.

"I'm Laurette with Southeast Alaska Maritime. Our van is right here, so we can follow the ambulance to the hospital."

The flustered woman looked at her in confusion.

Another seaman approached with a small suitcase. "We had her pack a few things," he explained to Laurette.

Grabbing the bag with one hand, Laurette put her other hand under the lady's elbow. "Come with me," she said softly. She led the woman up the ramp behind the patient. The medics handled the portable oxygen and IV bags. "Your husband is in good hands."

After stowing the suitcase in the back of the van, she made sure her passenger had buckled up. "We'll be at the hospital in a few minutes. May I ask your name?"

"I'm Gladys Sutherland. Dan had a heart attack." Her voice quivered.

"We'll take good care of both of you."

At the hospital, Laurette parked the van and led Mrs. Sutherland into the emergency waiting area. "You have a patient from a cruise ship. This is his wife," she told the nurse behind the desk. "Should we wait here for information about him?"

"We'll need some forms filled out. Can you do that?" The nurse looked at the flustered woman with Laurette.

"Let me help." Laurette coaxed Mrs. Sutherland to a seat and went back to pick up the clipboard. Efficiently, she got the information to fill in the necessary facts.

"I want to see Dan. Can you find out how he is?" Mrs. Sutherland pleaded.

Taking the papers back to the desk, Laurette asked, "Where will Mr. Sutherland be taken? How soon will his wife be able to see him?"

"Thank you," the admitting nurse said, taking the clipboard. "I'm sure the patient will go into the ICU. The nurse there will tell you when he can have visitors. Do you know where that waiting room is?"

Laurette shook her head.

"Let me take you up there and make sure there's a fresh pot of coffee."

Mrs. Sutherland seemed to be a bit more relaxed. "You are very kind," she told Laurette as they followed the nurse to the waiting room.

"They'll take good care of your husband. Everything will be all right." Laurette patted the woman's arm.

Gladys smiled weakly. "You make it all sound so possible."

"All things are possible with God." The nurse left them, and Laurette poured two cups of coffee. "Do you take anything in your coffee?"

"No, thank you." Mrs. Sutherland wrapped her hands around the cup.

"Are you cold? I could get you a blanket."

"Just shocked. It all happened so fast. Dan was fine at dinner. Said he had a little indigestion and wanted to go to bed early. Then he collapsed." She turned tear-filled eyes toward Laurette. "What am I going to do?"

Laurette put her arm around the weeping woman. "The doctors here are very good. The medics on board had your husband stabilized. If it had been more serious, he would have been flown in by helicopter. I'm sure they just want to monitor him for a day or two."

"But we live in Minnesota. How will we get home?"

Handing the woman a tissue, Laurette reassured her. "As soon as your husband is able to travel, we'll make arrangements for you to fly home. The cruise line will send your luggage to your house." She patted the distraught woman's shoulder. "Is there family you want to contact?"

"My son." She looked at Laurette. "Could I call my son?"

"Certainly. With the time difference, you won't even be waking him up. Let me find the nearest phone." Seeing the worried look on Mrs. Sutherland's face, she added, "I'll stay here while you call. If there's any news about your husband, I can let you know at once."

After reassurance from her son, Mrs. Sutherland relaxed a little. When the nurse came to tell her she could see her husband, she hugged Laurette and begged, "Will you please stay a little longer?"

"I'll be right here," she assured the worried woman. While she waited, Laurette pulled her Bible from her pack.

A short time later, Mrs. Sutherland returned looking much better. Her face held some color, and she had combed her hair. "They said as soon as Dan is out of intensive care, I can have a cot in his room." She sank into the chair next to Laurette. "All the tubes and wires look scary, but he talked to me. He says he's not in pain. The nurse taking care of him said they'll do more tests later today, but it doesn't look like there is new damage to his heart."

Laurette had closed her Bible with a silent prayer of thanks.

"Were you praying?" Mrs. Sutherland asked.

"Yes."

"Would you pray with me? I believed you when you told me all things are possible with God." She clasped Laurette's hand. "I'd feel better if we both prayed for Dan."

❧

Ryan had received Tyler's message when he returned from an evening of playing piano at the Dockside Hotel. He got to the office early and sent the two helpers out on the most critical tasks. He called the hospital to get a report on the heart attack victim and notified the ship's captain of the man's condition.

"They won't be able to rejoin the cruise. We'll see that they get a flight back home," Ryan told him.

"Understood. We'll take care of their luggage and see that it's shipped to them."

Taking over the office kept Ryan busy until late morning. He finally made it to the hospital to check on Laurette. She hadn't called in. "I'd better make sure the patient's wife is all right and see if Laurette needs help."

After checking at the front desk, he dashed to the waiting room. He paused at the door to watch the women. Laurette held the older lady's hand. He could see by the woman's expression that she was listening raptly to Laurette's words. "That girl is a charmer," he muttered.

Approaching the two, he noted the dark circles under Laurette's eyes. *Wonder if she got any sleep last night.*

Laurette jumped up when she saw him. "Are you looking for me?"

He smiled. "No. I only came to see if you needed help."

Laurette turned to her companion. "Gladys, this is my coworker, Ryan Nichols. Ryan, this is Mrs. Sutherland."

She stood to take Ryan's hand. "This girl has been with me ever since we got to the dock. I don't think I could have managed without her." Her look changed to one of concern. "She isn't in trouble for staying with me, is she?"

Ryan shook his head. "No, Mrs. Sutherland. Southeast Maritime is here to help you, and it looks like she has done a good job." He turned to Laurette. "Does Mrs. Sutherland have a place to stay?"

"They're letting her stay here. She can even get her meals here, so she never has to leave her husband. He's doing well, and I assured her we'll see that they get a flight home as soon as he can travel."

"Right. I let the ship's captain know so your friends on board will know you're all right," he told Mrs. Sutherland.

"I really should get back to work, Gladys, but I'll check on you later today." Ryan watched Laurette pick up her Bible and put it in her pack. "Maybe you could catch a nap while your husband's resting. You had a rough night."

"Thank you, dear. I'll try to do that. Would you pray with me again before you leave?"

Ryan stood back and watched as the women stood together and held hands. He heard Laurette's prayer and murmured "Amen" when the women did. *I've taken care of distraught family members before. This lady is calm and under control. Maybe there's something more to praying with another person than I realized,* he thought. Other than politely waiting while Laurette and Ruth said grace, he certainly hadn't done it recently. Not even alone. He'd have to give that some thought.

"I'll see you later," Laurette said, then gave Gladys a quick hug. "You ready to go?" she asked Ryan.

"You look beat," he said to Laurette as they exited the hospital. "How early did you get to the dock?"

"Oh, not until nearly four." She sighed. "Had a late night with Ruth."

"Is she okay?"

Laurette smiled up at him. "Just got her days and nights mixed up. I'll catch up on my sleep tonight."

"Come in late tomorrow. Tyler will be back, and we can struggle without you." Ryan longed to hug Laurette and comfort her. She did so much for others. Could he do anything for her?

"Thanks."

He walked her to the van she had left in the parking lot. "You want to stop for something to eat?"

She looked surprised. "Now that you mention it, I am hungry. I'll meet you at the coffee shop by the office."

He watched her drive off. "I wonder if she ever gets grouchy." He shrugged and walked to the company truck to follow her to the café.

six

"How's Ruth? Has she still got her days and nights mixed up?" Ryan asked when Laurette came into the office a few days later.

"She's been great for the last week. John came by Sunday. He even cooked dinner for us. He called it halibut cheeks. Do fish really have cheeks?"

She watched, embarrassed as Ryan's lean frame nearly doubled in laughter. Finally, he gasped out an answer. "Yes, Rette, halibut have cheeks. It's a delicacy."

Feeling a warm glow at hearing her nickname, she looked shyly at Ryan. "Sorry I had to ask. It tasted delicious, and I didn't want John to know how dumb I am."

His gaze softened. "I'm sure there are lots of things I wouldn't know about growing wheat. Sorry if my laughter made you uncomfortable."

"I like to see you happy. I'll try to ask more dumb questions." She smiled at him.

The phone rang and the fax machine rattled.

They had no more time to talk that day. By late afternoon, Laurette heaved a sigh of relief. The last ship had weighed anchor, and she could go home. Her stomach growled. Other than some pastry Tyler had brought back from one of the ships, she had not eaten since a bowl of cereal at five thirty that morning. She thought about all the groceries John had brought on Sunday. "Maybe I'll cook some pork chops," she muttered as she crossed the parking lot to her truck. "Oh, that doesn't look good." She changed her path and headed toward a couple on the dock. They stood where the tenders landed, and neither appeared happy.

"Hello, I'm Laurette with Southeast Alaska Maritime. Is there something I can help you with?"

The man turned to her. She could read the frustration on his face. "I told my wife the last tender left at three, but she insisted it was four. Now she won't believe me when I tell her that's our ship sailing out of the harbor."

"It's so pretty, Harold. I wish you'd take a picture."

"It is pretty. But I'm afraid your husband is right." Laurette kept her voice soft.

The look of surprise that came over the lady's face twisted Laurette's heart.

"I told you, Mabel, but you wouldn't listen." He looked at Laurette. "What can we do? Our luggage and our friends are on that ship." He waved his arm toward the departing vessel.

"Let me take you to the Dockside Hotel. You can stay there tonight, and we'll get you on a flight to your ship's next port of call. We should be able to get you on your way sometime tomorrow."

"Can you do that?" he asked, relief sweeping over his countenance.

"I don't like to fly," Mabel stated harshly.

"Come now, dear. It's all we can do, and this nice girl has offered to help us." He put his hand on his wife's arm and led her up the ramp to the street level.

"Do you see that building over there?" Laurette pointed to a large rustic building across the corner from the parking lot. "It's a nice hotel where you can be comfortable until we arrange for you to rejoin your ship."

"Why can't we take another boat out there now?" the woman asked with a frown.

"It would be a very rough ride in a small boat. Plus, you would have to climb a ladder on the side of your ship to get on board."

The lady smiled weakly. "How do we get to the hotel?"

"I'll take you there. It isn't far."

"I'm Harold Harris, and this is my wife, Mabel. I didn't catch your name, miss."

"I'm Laurette Martel." She had been walking slowly across the parking lot and now guided them across Harbor Drive to the Dockside Hotel. "The reservation desk is right there if you would like to sign for a room. I need to call my office," she told Mr. Harris. Pulling her cell phone out of her pocket, Laurette called the SAM office. Ryan answered. "I've got Mr. and Mrs. Harold Harris here at the Dockside Hotel. They didn't make it back to their ship before it sailed."

"Their ship's on its way to Vancouver, B.C. The Harrises will catch up with it in time to pick up their luggage and go home," he told her.

"Can't be helped. Should I call the airlines tonight?"

"I'll take care of it, and I'll notify the ship where they are. You get them settled at the hotel. Are they going to need medicine?"

"I'll ask and get back to you," she said, pushing the disconnect button.

She waited until Mr. Harris had finished at the desk and approached the couple. "What will you need?"

"The clerk says there are toiletries in the room, and if we need more to call." He smiled at his wife. "I guess you'll get to wear that sweatshirt you bought this afternoon." He pointed to the shopping bag she clutched.

"Do you take any prescription drugs that you will need right away?"

"I have it right here." Mrs. Harris dug into the large pocketbook she carried and pulled out a box with a compartment for each day's pills. "This kept getting lost in the suitcase, so I put it in my purse."

Laurette said a silent prayer of thanks. Getting medicine at this time of night could be a problem.

"Our office is in contact with your ship, so they'll know where you are. We should be able to make airline arrangements for tomorrow." She took a business card from her pocket. "If you need anything, please call my cell phone."

"Thank you, Laurette. You were an angel sent to help us." Mr. Harris squeezed her hand between both of his.

"We'll be in contact with you in the morning. I hope you have a pleasant night." Laurette watched the couple walk toward their room. She could smell food from the café. *The pork chops can wait.*

She went into the restaurant and drank a cola while the waitress made up take-out boxes of the nightly special. *Hope Ruth likes meat loaf,* she thought after paying for the food.

Laurette arrived home to smell fresh baking.

Ruth came to the kitchen door with a big smile. "I baked a cake."

"Smells good and looks better." Laurette put the take-out boxes next to the sheet cake on the table.

"I used one of the box things John left here. He even had a can of frosting to go with it. I hope it tastes all right."

"It will be wonderful." Laurette put the teakettle on the stove and took dishes from the cupboard. "I brought some hot food home. Then we'll have that dessert."

When Laurette said grace, she silently added thanks to Jesus for taking care of her friend. "Wow, Ruth. Your cake is almost too pretty to eat."

"When did you make meat loaf? I haven't had any in a long time. It tastes good."

Laurette told her friend about the people who missed their ship, explaining that the convenience of the take-out meal was too good to pass up. "I decided to let someone else do the cooking for us since I was running so late."

Ruth chuckled. "Nice to know I'm not the only one who

gets confused. And we ended up with a delicious dinner."

Ruth cut pieces of cake while Laurette refilled their cups. "When will we have Ryan over for dinner again?" she asked.

"I hadn't thought about it," Laurette admitted. "I asked him before because he was taking me to the music festival."

"Well, let's feed him again."

"I'll take him some cake tomorrow. That'll tempt him to come to dinner."

Ruth smiled. Laurette could see her friend's pleasure in the compliment.

"I'm not sure whether Ryan's a believer." Laurette sipped her tea.

"Do you talk to him about Jesus?"

"Not really. I don't know how to begin."

"Shouldn't be hard for you to talk about the Savior. Your faith is evident in all you do."

"Really?" Laurette looked closely at Ruth. She seemed so clearheaded tonight, and she had baked a cake. She dared to hope it would last. *Please, Jesus, hold Your servant Ruth in love and guidance.*

"Shall we get these dishes cleaned up?" Ruth started to stack the plates.

After they had washed the dishes together, Ruth settled in her chair while Laurette e-mailed her parents. She knew her dad and brother would be busy with the wheat harvest. Her mom would be cooking huge meals to feed the workers. A note from their daughter would assure them she was okay.

"Ready to read now?" Ruth asked when Laurette closed her laptop.

After sharing the Scriptures, the women prepared for bed. Laurette had just reached for the light in her room when her cell phone rang.

"Did I wake you?" Ryan asked.

"No. When the phone rang, I was afraid it was the couple

I left at the hotel."

"Just me. How did you come to find those people?"

"I saw them standing on the dock and went to see if I could help."

"You do have a way of finding the lost. Anyway, the airlines just called and the Harrises have a reservation on the tomorrow afternoon flight."

"Are you still at the office?" she asked in alarm. His low laugh stirred a new feeling in her heart.

"The airlines called me at home. Sorry if I bothered you."

"No bother. I was worried about you working so late."

"Thanks for caring. See you in the morning."

❧

Ryan put the phone down. *That girl can bring sunshine to the darkest gloom. Even her voice sparkles. And she's worried about how late I worked. Always concerned about others. . .*

He picked up the box he had taken out of the spare bedroom. He had found the hymnbook he wanted. He also picked up his Bible. "I won this for perfect attendance," he muttered. He knew he didn't deserve it; he just went with Mom, and she had to be there every week to play the hymns. He left the Bible on the living room table and put the hymnal on the small organ that stood against the wall. He and his mother had both cried when she sold the baby grand. But she had left him the organ.

Sitting down and turning on the instrument, Ryan flipped pages and played some of the hymns his mother used to play. His mind tossed out memories of his boyhood. The house was always full of music. Mom either practiced the piano or gave lessons, or the stereo sent music wafting throughout the house. Mom got lost in her music after Dad died. He recalled her joy after she met Harvey. "Why did I dislike him?" Ryan asked himself.

Maybe you were jealous when she shared her love of music with someone besides you, his conscience nagged.

"Give your bitterness to Jesus." Laurette's voice echoed in his mind. He silently read the words to the music his fingers produced. *"Sin sick and sorrow worn, whom Christ doth heal."*

"I wasn't fair to Mom. She found happiness and I tried to stand in her way."

The commandment to honor one's parents flashed through his mind. "I'm full of sin. Could Christ heal me?"

Absently he turned the organ off, walked back to the table, and picked up the Bible. "I don't even know where to start." He let the book fall open and started reading; Psalm 25:7 caught his eye. He read it to himself twice, then read it aloud.

" 'Remember not the sins of my youth, nor my transgressions: according to thy mercy remember thou me for thy goodness' sake, O Lord.' Hmm. Is the psalmist asking God to remember him in love, not for his past sins?"

The words stayed with Ryan as he put the Bible back on the table before he carried the box back to the spare room closet. "That isn't how I've been remembering my mom," he admitted, wondering what Laurette would say about that.

Ryan went to the phone, pausing briefly before calling Tyler at home. He respected Tyler and knew the man would give him a straight answer. Ryan grinned. Then Tyler would probably tell him to double check with his pastor, just to be sure.

⋅᷷⋅

The next morning, the office was even more hectic than usual. Tyler had gone to sort out a freight problem. Laurette left a message that she had gone to the Dockside Hotel to check on the Harrises and assure them she would take them to the airport in the afternoon. Thoughts of trying to talk to Rette had vanished from Ryan's mind.

"You have to take this call," Debbie told him.

Ryan listened to the request and went numb. His mind refused to work. "How many tanks do you need?" he asked.

"I'll see what I can do and get back to you." He put the phone down and watched Laurette come in the door and head for the coffeepot.

"You look like you lost your last friend," she commented, offering to fill his cup.

"Just my job," he muttered, taking the proffered coffee. "I need to find someplace to fill those small oxygen tanks people pull around."

"So what's the problem?" Laurette sipped her coffee.

"Where do I get twenty oxygen tanks filled?"

"How about the hospital? Maybe they have a supply of tanks or source to fill them."

Ryan felt like a ton of weight had been lifted off his chest. "Of course. They deal with oxygen tanks for patients all the time. You're my savior."

"No, Jesus is your Savior."

"Actually, I'd like to talk to you about that later. But I've got some calls to make."

"Ruth wants you to come to dinner."

"Only Ruth?" He stopped on his way to the phone.

Laurette's smile warmed him clear down to his toes. "We'll both welcome the chance to talk with you about Jesus. Can you come to dinner tomorrow night?"

"You've got a date." Ryan made a call and settled the oxygen tank arrangements.

"Can they do it?" Laurette asked when he hung up the phone.

"Yes. You've made a lot of passengers breathe easier."

He laughed at her grimace. "Okay, so it was a bad pun. What time tomorrow?"

"I'll look at our schedule and tell you later."

"Leave me a note. I'm off to collect some oxygen bottles."

Is it her faith in God that keeps her so cheerful? I'm going to find out if He can do that for me, Ryan vowed, jumping aboard the tender.

seven

Laurette stopped by the grocery store on her way home. "I don't have time to fix a fancy meal," she murmured, picking up hamburger and bottled spaghetti sauce. "I can fix this quick before Ryan gets to the house tomorrow night." Thankful for her neoprene rain gear, she pulled up the hood and carried the groceries to her truck.

With the windshield wipers going full blast, Laurette drove home, thinking about the e-mail she'd received from her parents. Her mother kept track of the weather in Sitka and worried that Laurette would be depressed with all the rain. *Your father says nothing would get you down, but I think the weather could.* She was still thinking about her parents when she pulled into the driveway.

Pleasant memories of her loving parents vanished. Ruth stood on the deck wearing her housedress—no coat—watering her flowers. Laurette pulled up her hood and hurried to Ruth's side.

"Welcome home. I'm just fertilizing my geraniums," Ruth explained.

Trying to smile, Laurette took the watering can and guided Ruth back in the house. "Please get out of your wet clothes. I have to bring some groceries in from the truck."

Rushing to complete her task and get the ice cream in the freezer, Laurette made it back before Ruth had taken her dress off.

"I'm going to run you a hot bath. You're soaked to the skin and might catch cold." She coaxed Ruth from the kitchen, where she stood dripping water on the floor.

"The floor's wet." Ruth began to shiver.

"I'll mop it up later. Right now we need to get you warm again."

Moments later, she helped Ruth step into the bathtub. "How's that? Warm enough?"

Ruth nodded. "I always fertilize the flowers on Monday."

Laurette didn't have the heart to tell her it was Thursday. "Are you warm now?" she asked a few minutes later.

"Yes, dear, but why do I have to put on my nightgown?" she asked as Laurette helped her dry off and dress.

"It will keep you warm." She handed Ruth her robe and set her slippers on the floor for her to step into. "Why don't you go sit in your chair while I pick up your wet clothes."

Once the floor had been wiped dry and the wet clothes put in the washer, Laurette opened the refrigerator. "I give up," she sighed. After packaging the pork chops, she labeled them and put them in the freezer. Next she measured water to boil for an instant noodle soup. "This will warm Ruth on the inside." She put the teakettle on to boil and sliced some cheese to go with the crackers she had put on a plate.

"Would you like to come to the table, or should I set up a tray?"

"No need for that fuss. I'll come to the supper table."

Ruth liked the noodles and ate well. "Do we still have some cake?"

Laurette poured hot water into the teapot. "Sure do. This tea will be ready in a few minutes to go with it."

"I invited Ryan to come to dinner tomorrow night." Laurette put a slice of cake in front of her friend. At least Ruth remembered baking. "There is still cake and I bought ice cream to go with it."

"Doesn't he like chocolate milk?" Ruth asked.

Now why would she remember something like that and still stand in the rain until her clothes were soaked? "Yes, I bought some of that, too. You go ahead and relax. I'll clean up the kitchen."

"All right." Ruth went back to her chair. "Will you read to me later?"

"Of course." Laurette tossed the washed clothes into the dryer before starting on the dishes. *Please, Jesus, show me how to take care of this sweet lady. I place her in Your protection,* Laurette prayed as she put the dishes away.

ъ

The next morning the office staff laughed when Laurette described Ruth watering flowers in the rain. Ryan sipped his coffee thoughtfully and did not join in the merriment. He noted that Rette seemed uncomfortable with her coworkers' jokes. "She really loves that sweet old lady," he murmured before draining his cup.

Ryan wondered if he should talk to John to find out if he knew how bad his mother's mind was getting. Taking care of Ruth might become too much for Rette. He shoved such thoughts to the back of his mind and started assigning tasks for the day. Tyler had been called to supervise the loading of a log ship in Hyder and left Ryan in charge.

The gray day matched Ryan's mood until it was time to leave the office. The closer he got to Rette's house, the more his spirits lifted. After hanging his raincoat in the outer room and kicking off his waterproof boots, Ryan entered the cheery kitchen. Ruth looked up from putting plates on the table. Rette turned from stirring a bubbling pot on the stove.

"Welcome," Laurette said, putting down her spoon. "Almost ready. I just need to toss a salad."

"It's nice to have you back," Ruth added.

Ryan handed Ruth a small bunch of flowers he had purchased at the grocery. "To my favorite girlfriend," he teased.

Ruth rewarded him with a glowing smile. "What a thoughtful boy. Do we have something to put these in?" she asked Laurette.

Wouldn't she know what was in her own house? Ryan wondered. He watched Rette take down a glass vase for her.

Ruth fussed with the flowers as though they were the finest roses. "I do love flowers," she said with a bright smile.

Enough to stand in the rain to feed them, he thought. "I'm glad you like them. Can I help?" he asked Rette.

She put a bowl of green salad on the table. "Just find a seat, and I'll bring over the food."

Ryan seated Ruth in her favorite spot. Then he watched Rette take garlic bread from the oven before placing a bowl of spaghetti in front of him. "Smells good," he told her.

The three held hands while Ruth said grace.

The food tasted as good as it smelled. "I'm hungry. Didn't have time for lunch today."

"Too often you make do with a carton of milk," Laurette scolded him.

He grinned as he took another piece of bread. "I like it when you worry about me. Maybe you'll cook for me more often."

"I like to have you eat with us," Ruth said. "Laurette fixes me a nice supper every night, and it's fun to share."

"And Ruth baked a cake," Laurette said, getting up to make a pot of tea. "Would you like more milk?" she asked Ryan.

"Sure, I'll have some with Ruth's cake." He rose and helped her clear the table.

≈

Ryan relaxed in the warm atmosphere. He pushed back his empty dessert plate and patted his stomach. "Best meal I've had in weeks."

"That's because you live on junk food," Laurette accused.

"Let's get the dishes done so you can read to me," Ruth suggested. She turned to Ryan. "Laurette reads the Bible to me every night. Sometimes we talk about the things she reads."

"I tried to read the Bible, but I don't know where to start." Ryan put a stack of dirty dishes next to the sink.

Ruth beamed. "You're welcome to join us. We learn something every day."

Ruth's childlike manner charmed Ryan. He could understand why Rette was so protective of this sweet old lady.

"How about if Rette and I do the dishes?" At her nod, Ryan offered to escort Ruth to the living room. He settled her in her chair and tucked a lap robe around her legs.

He stopped in the kitchen doorway. Rette bustled about, putting the food away. The overhead light made her cap of curly hair shine, tempting him to run his fingers through the chestnut tangles. She had changed from her work clothes into plain gray sweats. In his eyes, she was beautiful.

She caught him watching her and blushed. "Will you dry the dishes for me?"

"Thought you'd never ask." He picked up the dish towel.

"You're welcome to stay while I read to Ruth, but please don't feel obligated." She looked up at him, her gaze begging for understanding. "It's become a habit, and she loves it."

"Don't you think I could learn something?" He put down the plate he held. "Rette, you're different. You're always upbeat, kind, and understanding. I don't think I've ever seen you lose your cool. Is it your faith that gives you that positive attitude?"

She stood with her hands in the soapy water. "I love Jesus and trust Him to take care of me." She looked up with a lopsided smile. "I do get upset. Usually it's with myself for not giving a problem to Him and leaving it there. I try to take it back and solve it myself. Doesn't work that way," she explained.

"Isn't it selfish to ask Him to take on my problems? How can I feel good about doing that?"

"When we have tasks at work, you assign them to someone

else. That's not being selfish. Can't you think of it as delegating your life problems to Jesus?"

"Seems kind of presumptuous if not hypocritical for me to say to Him, 'I've kind of ignored You for a long time, Lord, but now I want to dump my problems on You, okay?' Don't you think?" He picked up another plate to dry.

"Maybe you could just talk to Him."

"You mean pray?"

"Yes, you could call it that. I just carry on a conversation with Him. Jesus is my friend."

"I don't know Him well—you know, intimately. I accepted Him as my Savior when I was a child, but I never took the time to get close. Not real proud of that. I think that makes it harder now. I've got no excuses."

"That's what forgiveness is all about, Ryan. Get to know Jesus Christ. Learn to trust Him and your life will never be the same."

"I still don't know where to begin," Ryan said quietly. His heart beat in double time. *Am I ready for this?*

"I'd like to share my faith with you."

Her voice held warmth that sent a glow through him.

Laurette dried her hands on the edge of the towel he held. "Let's get started." She took the stack of plates he'd dried and put them in the cupboard.

Ruth dozed in her chair but perked up when they joined her. "I have the books right here." She patted the end table next to her chair.

Laurette held out a small pamphlet. Ryan took it, wondering what it had to do with reading the Bible.

"This is the daily guide we've been following. There are lots of different ones. Ruth likes this one; it's published quarterly. Every day there are readings from the Old Testament, New Testament, and Psalms. Then there is a short devotional based on one of the Scriptures."

"So you don't just let the Bible fall open and read that page," Ryan said respectfully.

"I suppose some people do, but some like to know where they're going." She smiled at Ruth. "We read the psalm last because that's Ruth's favorite part. We don't always stop with one."

"The Psalms are songs, Ryan. You should like that," Ruth interjected. "I can always find something in Psalms that fits my feelings."

Ryan wanted to know more but feared embarrassment at showing how little he knew. "Okay, I'm ready."

Rette opened the devotional book and flipped open the Bible to the readings for the day.

Ryan cringed at how easily she found the chapters. She looked at him with a gentle smile. "Comes from lots of practice."

Ryan listened to her soft voice as she read the Scriptures. *Never sounded like that when I went to church,* he thought. He watched Ruth. She looked like a cherub, and her wrinkled cheeks were flushed with warmth and joy. He doubted her mind would ever get too dull to enjoy the Bible.

Laurette read for several minutes, then turned to Ryan. "Do you have a Bible?"

He nodded but was not about to tell her he'd won it at church years ago.

"Some people start out reading Psalms every day. I've found all sorts of human experiences in those pages. Joy, yearning, serenity, and anger—it's all there."

"And that's how you learn about God?"

"What better way than reading how the people of Psalms wept together, danced together, and celebrated hope together in God. Ruth's right; they are songs. Let their melody lead you to a new life."

Ryan noticed that Ruth had nodded off. *I should get out of here so she can go to bed.* "I've enjoyed myself," he told the ladies. "Thank you for dinner." He rose from his chair.

"I'll walk you out." Laurette followed him through the kitchen. "Thank you for being so good to Ruth," she said as he took down his raincoat.

"I can see why you worry about her. She shouldn't be alone all day."

"Someone from her church calls at ten every morning. At least a couple times a week, one of her friends from there comes to visit. I know John is worried. As long as I'm here, she can stay in her home a little longer."

Her deep sigh tugged at him. "Don't try to do too much." He fought the urge to comfort her with a hug. Instead, he bent over to pull on his boots. Standing upright again, he said, "Hey, I checked the schedule and next Wednesday we have an afternoon off. The only ship in port sails at noon. Would you like to go fishing?"

"I've never fished in the ocean. I wouldn't know what to do."

"You gave me tips on how to navigate the Bible tonight. How about if I show you how to navigate a fishing pole next week?"

She rewarded him with a brilliant smile. "It's a deal."

eight

Laurette stood in the doorway until Ryan's Volkswagen disappeared down the driveway. Turning back into the house, she heard Ruth getting ready for bed. She went over to the big window overlooking the water, then sat on the window seat and hugged her knees to her chest. The heavy gray clouds seemed to touch the water over the channel; it wouldn't stay light until nearly midnight tonight as it usually did during the Alaskan summer.

A pair of eagles drifted in lazy circles on the air currents above the water. Laurette's spirits seemed to soar with the birds. Could it be true? Ryan seemed genuinely interested in learning more about the Bible. She really liked Ryan, but she could never be serious about a man who did not believe in Jesus. While he said he'd accepted Jesus as a child, he didn't live his life like a believer with a strong faith—he'd admitted as much this evening. Would he someday choose to turn back to God?

She remembered how gentle and kind he had been toward Ruth. *He isn't the same grouch who met my plane a few weeks ago. Maybe I misjudged him.* Suddenly she recalled how disappointed Ryan had seemed that day when Jenny hadn't returned to Sitka. Later, when Laurette e-mailed Jenny to see how her dad was doing, her friend had confirmed that she and Ryan had only dated casually, that nothing serious had developed. Now Laurette wondered if his disappointment was subconsciously more about his mother not returning than about Jenny.

Where can this friendship go? her conscience nagged. *Your job only lasts until fall. Then what are you going to do?*

She shivered at the thought. Would she go back to Washington to look for a job? That's what her folks would expect her to do. Sighing deeply, Laurette stood up. *I'll have to pray for guidance. And for Ryan.* Whatever happened between them, it was more important what happened between Ryan and the Lord.

The sliver of light shining under Ruth's bedroom door had gone out, so Laurette entered her room and prepared for bed. Thoughts of Ryan and the future kept her tossing for hours before she fell into a deep sleep.

❦

Wednesday dawned bright and sunny. "Great day to go fishing," Tyler commented when he heard about Ryan and Laurette's plans. "You can use the company truck to launch your boat," he told Ryan. "I'm taking the van this afternoon."

Laurette went home to change into jeans and a sweatshirt. She made sure Ruth was settled. Diane had promised to call that evening and remind Ruth to eat the supper Laurette had left for her when she'd made the sandwiches for their lunch. Ryan was bringing the soft drinks and potato chips.

Carrying their lunch and her jacket, she walked from her truck to the launch site near the dock where the tenders landed. Ryan had his boat lined up at the top of the ramp and was ready to back down.

"Can I help?" she asked.

"When the boat floats off the trailer, will you grab the bow rope and hold on?"

Laurette nodded and walked down to where she could reach the rope tied to the bow of the white wooden craft. "You have a nice boat," she commented.

"It was my dad's. It's old, but it floats."

She smiled. "That's good." Laurette watched as he backed the boat and trailer into the water. *Hope I don't get seasick,* she worried to herself as she kept a firm grip on the rope. When the boat floated free, she pulled it toward the dock and held on to the side.

"You did that like a pro," Ryan said when he returned from parking the truck and trailer. "Are you ready to go?"

"I guess so." She climbed into the boat and sat in the passenger seat.

Ryan took the other seat and started the outboard motor, then steered them out of the harbor.

Laurette looked around her. The sun sparkled on the blue water, making her glad she had worn sunglasses. "It's beautiful," she said in awe. The boat moved slowly until Ryan cleared the harbor. When he opened the throttle, she held on to the bar in front of her seat and glanced at the wake breaking in a white froth behind them. Ryan poked her arm and pointed up.

Laurette counted six eagles circling in the bright blue sky above them. She nodded to acknowledge she'd seen them, since the loud motor made it impossible to talk. The wind whipped across her face, and a faint, cool spray rose alongside the boat as the hull cut through the swells. Excitement filled her. She leaned forward to see over the bow and turned to smile at Ryan. She couldn't read his expression and was too full of joy to try to figure it out.

Suddenly he reached for the throttle and slowed the motor. He looked down at her, then pointed ahead and to the right.

She quickly stood beside him. "Oh," was all she could say when she saw the spout of water.

"Killer whales," Ryan explained.

"I can hear them blow," she whispered in awe. "How many are there?"

He shook his head. "Hard to say. At least three," he said as an enormous black whale breached the surface. As it turned, she saw its white underbelly markings.

Laurette watched in wonder as the whale seemed to dance

on its tail before falling back in the water with a loud crash.

"That's one impressive belly flop!"

Ryan laughed. "They're going to put on a show for you."

She had heard several ships' captains call over the radio that they would anchor late since they'd stopped for the passengers to watch the whales. One of the whales flipped its enormous tail in the air and smashed it against the water, making a sound like a cannon.

"It reminds me of the story of Jonah. When I heard the story as a kid, I could not believe there was a sea creature big enough to swallow a man." She smiled at Ryan before turning back to watch the whales. "They're beautiful beyond belief," she said in fascination as the whales moved on, their telltale spouting getting farther away.

Ryan put the motor back in gear. "We'll fish over by those rocks," Ryan pointed.

"Will the whales come back?" Laurette asked, fearing the whales would come dangerously close to their craft.

"They eat a lot of fish, so we'll need to find another spot if we want to catch any."

Ryan stopped the engine a few minutes later. "I'll start the trolling motor. The outboard is much louder, and it's easier to fish creeping along slowly with a less powerful motor," he explained, moving to the stern and lowering the propeller shaft of a small motor into the water.

Laurette watched as he pull started it and settled against one corner of the stern to steer.

"Think you could steer this?" Ryan asked. "Then I can get the poles rigged and ready to fish."

"Okay." Laurette moved cautiously toward him.

"Put a cushion behind you for comfort," Ryan instructed as she leaned her back into the corner he'd vacated. "Push left to go right, and right to go left. Twist the handle here to adjust the throttle. Practice a little to get comfortable with it. But wait until I sit down," he added with a grin.

Laurette took the handle and tried to see where they were going. "Where do I head?"

"Just keep us from hitting anyone." Ryan grinned again and pulled a fishing pole from the shelf below the gunwale on her side of the boat.

Laurette pushed the handle to get the boat to go the way she wanted, taking a few minutes to get used to the feeling. She breathed a quick prayer of thanks that there were no other boats in the area at the moment.

"Ready to go." Ryan held a pole over the side and let the line out. "This one will be yours," he announced, putting the pole in a holder mounted on the gunwale. "When you hear line going out and see the pole bouncing, you've got a fish."

Laurette gulped and nodded. She was still struggling with turning left and right. Now she was supposed to watch for boats and catch fish, too? *I thought this would be fun.*

Ryan soon had another pole ready and put it in the holder next to her. "Don't worry. You'll get used to it. I'll take over now. You can go back to the seat up front and watch your pole."

Sighing in relief, Laurette did as she was told. She stared at the pole for a while, watching it bounce with the rhythm of the motor. The sparkling water, the warm sun, and the gentle rocking sensation made her drowsy. She'd almost dozed off when the movement of her pole snapped her alert.

"Fish on!" Ryan shouted, shutting down the motor. "Grab that pole."

Laurette lunged for his now empty seat at the stern and struggled to pull his pole out of its holder.

❧

Ryan watched her. "You've got it. Now keep the tip of the pole in the air and slowly move it toward the water, reeling as you go." He stood close behind her, speaking softly. "Now pull the pole back up straight. Then you're pulling the fish in."

Laurette looked up at him with a shining smile that touched his heart. She kept pumping the fishing pole up and down and reeling in line until a large silver fish jumped out of the water.

"Oh, have I lost him?"

"No, he's just taking a look at us." When the reel spun out more line, he put his hand on Laurette's shoulder. "Let him run. When he's tired it'll be easier to get him in the boat."

Ryan looked at the concentration showing in Laurette's face. He smiled and continued to encourage her while she fought the fish. When he saw the fish coming in again, he reached for the handle of the net. "Keep reeling him in." He moved next to Laurette at the stern. "When you see the weight on your line coming out of the water, stop reeling. Hold the pole up so the line stays tight, and bring the fish toward me. I'll have him netted in no time."

He slipped the net under the salmon and brought it into the boat. The look of wonder and joy on Laurette's face filled him with warmth. She put her hand up for a high five. Ryan fought the urge to pull her into his arms. Instead, he clapped hands with her, shouting, "Well done!"

He pulled the hooks from the salmon's mouth and held it up for Laurette to see. "This your first?"

"Yes."

Her look of astonishment made him smile. "You're a born fisherman. Time to get the hooks baited and catch some more." He dropped the salmon into the cooler. "I can't let you outfish me." Ryan couldn't resist putting his arm around her shoulders. Her upturned face and glowing countenance made it hard to resist kissing her.

What's wrong with me? he scolded himself, turning away to pick up the net. *I work with this girl. I can't be treating her like a girlfriend.*

Why not? he countered. *I'm attracted to her.*

And she's going to leave at the end of summer.

"Will you show me how to bait my hook?" Laurette asked, interrupting his warring thoughts.

Bending close to Rette, showing her how to maneuver the small baitfish onto the hook, he pushed his conflicting thoughts aside. He soaked up her excitement. When she looked up at him, he thought he read the same feelings in her eyes.

Could it happen? Could she care for him?

The baited hooks went back into the water and they let out their lines. Ryan smiled to himself seeing how hard Laurette concentrated on her fishing pole.

Before long she had another fish. He stood by, coaching her. This time when the fish jumped, it spit the hook out. "You can't catch them all." She looked so sad he wanted to kiss her more than ever.

Behave! his conscience screamed. *She's too nice a girl to have you romancing her. You have no future that could include a girlfriend.*

"Let me try to bait the hook myself," Laurette begged.

Ryan backed off. He handed her a herring and watched her struggle to follow the directions he had given her the first time. She was determined; he'd give her that.

"Is that okay?" She held the line and baited hook up for his inspection.

"Go for it. Put your line out eighteen pulls."

He had the trolling motor going and his own line in the water. He watched as she carefully counted the pulls from the reel to the first eye in the pole.

Laurette stood at the stern. "What's that mountain over there? It looks like Fuji in Japan."

"It's Mt. Edgecumbe. Everyone thinks it looks like Fuji. Would you like to climb it sometime?"

"No, I've never climbed a mountain," she protested.

Ryan chuckled. "It's an easy hike. Have to take a boat to the island. There's a cabin there, and the path starts right behind it. We could do it in a day."

"I've done a little hiking, so I think I could manage."

"We'll keep an eye on the schedule and see when we could get some time off—hey, fish on!" Ryan grabbed his pole and started reeling his fish in. "Think you can net this?"

"Will you make me swim home if I miss?" Laurette teased.

"No. Just do your best." As the fish came closer to the boat, he explained when to dip the net in front of the salmon. After he guided the fish into it, he helped Laurette pull net and fish into the boat.

"We're a great team!" she shouted, giving him another high five.

They ate their sandwiches in between catching fish, but part of Laurette's got tossed overboard in her excitement to get to her pole. Then she stepped back so Ryan could net her fish and knocked his can of pop over.

"You're dangerous," Ryan teased. Her glow of pride when he held up her catch made him laugh. "But you sure can fish."

"It's getting late!" Laurette exclaimed, looking at her watch.

Ryan didn't want the day to end. "I suppose we should be starting back. Think you could steer us toward the harbor?"

"If you point the way."

They brought the fishing lines back into the boat and stowed the gear. Ryan pulled the trolling motor up, secured the bracket, and came back to the driver's seat to start the outboard engine. He motioned Laurette to get in his seat and take the wheel, then showed her how to operate the controls. He pointed to a rock formation and spoke in her ear. "Keep heading for the rocks."

He went back to the stern, where he started cleaning the fish. He kept an eye on Laurette and made sure she kept them headed in the right direction.

"Want me to take over?" he shouted, coming up behind her.

She smiled, slowed to a stop, and took the engine out of gear, then slid over to the passenger seat. Ryan took them back to the harbor.

"Will you hold the boat at the dock while I go get the truck and trailer?"

Laurette nodded.

He had launched and trailered his boat by himself enough times that he never worried. He didn't need to. Laurette seemed to know exactly what to do to help him. They soon had the boat secured on the trailer in the parking lot, ready to go.

Laurette took the bag of fish he held out to her. "Can you cook as well as you catch?" he asked, grinning.

"To prove it, Ruth and I will have you over for dinner."

"Sounds good to me."

"It's been a wonderful day. Thanks for taking me fishing." Before he could react, Laurette stood on tiptoe and brushed his cheek with her lips.

His mouth went dry and his heart raced. He mutely watched her slip away and head for her truck.

nine

Laurette drove toward home, marveling once again that even though the sun still shone bright, it was after 10:00 p.m. *Ryan still has to take his boat home and clean it. He'll be tired tomorrow.* Thoughts of Ryan sent her spirits soaring. She felt her face heat at the remembered kiss. *Will he think me too forward? He's my coworker. I'd better be more careful,* she cautioned herself.

She entered the quiet house and put the fish in the kitchen sink. "Better get these packaged and put away," she muttered. "I'll save this nice fillet to cook for Ryan." Laurette felt she worked efficiently for someone who'd had no idea what a fresh-caught salmon looked like a few hours ago. When the fish had been packaged and put in the freezer, she stretched and decided on a quick shower before bed.

Tired as she felt, sleep did not come at once. Thoughts of Ryan raced through her mind. The day had indeed been special. She'd never had a companion like him before.

Is he more than a friend? Sighing, she pulled the covers up and prayed silently until she fell asleep.

❧

Being around Ryan at work did not become a problem. They were so busy, they didn't have time for personal talk.

On Sunday, when Laurette returned from an errand, Debbie put down the phone and handed her a message. "Tyler has a meeting with a cruise director, and Ryan left this."

> *Take time for church. We can handle things until you get back.*
>
> Ryan

Looking up from the note, Laurette asked, "Where is Ryan?"

"Had to pick up some freight and take it out in the company boat," Debbie answered.

"His message says I can take a couple hours off for church."

Debbie looked puzzled. "Never knew Ryan to worry about church before." She shrugged. "Go ahead. I can handle things here."

❧

The service had started, but Laurette spotted Diane and slid into the seat beside her.

Diane smiled and patted Laurette's hand. "Nice to see you," she whispered.

After church, Diane coaxed Laurette to go with her to pick up the children from Sunday school. "They'd love to see you," she said.

Soon the children scampered around her, vying for Laurette's attention.

"They get lonesome in the summer. Tyler is hardly ever home, and when I'm not teaching, they don't get to go to day care or school. Maybe you could come by the house for lunch."

"I should get back, but I would like to talk to you about Ruth, and John is gone again."

"Is she getting worse?" Diane grabbed David and pulled him back from playing in the dirt in the parking lot. Turning to Laurette, she asked, "Can't you come by the house for a few minutes?"

Laurette agreed and followed Diane home. She shouldn't be away long, but she needed to talk to someone about Ruth.

Over cups of tea and the din of two excited children, Laurette told Diane about Ruth's latest mishaps. "I worry about her. She's so dear, but I can't be there all the time."

"Let's keep praying for her. She should be able to stay at

home as long as she doesn't do something drastic." Diane smiled. "And as long as you stay there."

"My job with SAM will end in the fall. I don't know what I'll do then. My parents will expect me to come back to Washington and find a job."

"You could get a job teaching at our church school."

"I majored in biology. I do plants, not children," Laurette protested. "And I don't really have a reason to stay in Sitka."

Diane raised her eyebrows but said nothing. "How was your fishing trip?"

Laurette felt the excitement rush through her as she told her friend about the day with Ryan. "I hope I can go again."

"I'm sure he'll manage to take you out fishing again. How about checking your schedule and you and I going out to lunch next week? You need to see more of Sitka than Crescent Harbor."

"That would be great, but I should get back to work now or I won't have a job. Call me later about lunch?"

❧

She saw Ryan in the office when she got back. "Sorry I took so long. I went home with Diane and the children."

"No problem. It's hard on her in the summer, and it seems the head office is asking Tyler to be on the road more and more often."

"Which means more work for you."

"We all help with what has to be done. Especially you. I'm not in this alone."

Laurette felt her face burn at the compliment. "When can you find time to come for that salmon dinner?"

"You ever cooked salmon?"

"No, but I'm sure I can learn. Maybe Ruth will be able to tell me what to do."

Laurette laughed at Ryan's look of concern.

"You'd better get a cookbook. Better yet, does she have a

barbecue? I can come cook for you," Ryan offered.

"Sounds good. Name the day."

The phone rang and Debbie shouted for Ryan. He gave Laurette a quick hug as he went by her on the way to the next office and the waiting call. "I'll get back to you."

His touch sent tingles down her spine.

❧

It was after seven before Ryan left the office. Too tired to cook, he'd stuck a frozen meal in the microwave and plopped down in the one easy chair in his small living room. Wrinkling his nose, he put down the TV dinner and drank a quart of chocolate milk. Lying back in his chair, he listened to music. He always turned on the stereo as soon as he came through the door. Mozart drifted on the air and soothed his weary mind.

He looked at the clock. "Too late to call Mom." It surprised him, but he wanted to talk to her. She'd given him the money to buy his own place. It wasn't much, but it was home. She'd also insisted he keep the organ so he had an instrument to play. And he'd never told her he played at the Dockside Hotel.

You didn't want her to know how much you miss the baby grand, his conscience reminded him.

It's time I did something different with my life. Laurette was right when she said I should stop being bitter. It'd be nice to have a future with her. He heaved himself out of the chair. Before he could think about her seriously, he should be able to offer her something. He didn't think his run-down trailer was her style. He stuffed the uneaten TV dinner in the garbage, picked up a bag of dirty laundry, and headed out the door. *I don't even have a washing machine.* He paused at the door and went back to pick up his Bible. He could at least read while he did his laundry. The door banged behind him.

❧

Dinner was over and Laurette had read until Ruth started to fall asleep. As long as she knew whether it was day or night, she did okay. "Hard to tell," Laurette muttered, looking out on bright daylight as the clock neared nine thirty. The phone interrupted her thoughts.

"Hi," Diane greeted Laurette. "Called to make a date for lunch. Time you played tourist and went sightseeing."

"You know, I haven't even been to the Russian Church yet."

"We'll do that, and the kids will want to climb to Castle Hill. David likes to see the cannons."

"How far do I have to climb?"

"If the kids can do it, you can. It's just a path up to where Baranof's castle used to be. Take your camera."

"Okay," Laurette agreed. "My mother keeps asking for pictures, and I haven't taken a roll of film since I've been here."

❧

Diane came by the office the next day, and the children climbed all over their father. "Do I have to give Laurette the afternoon off to get you guys to let me work?" Tyler teased.

"Yup!" David announced. "I want to see the cannons."

Tyler tossed his son in the air before putting him down and mussing Katie's hair. He escorted his wife and children to the office door, where he gave Diane a quick kiss. Laurette followed the rowdy children down the hall. They grabbed her hands and hurried her down the steps.

After sandwiches at the coffee shop, the group headed for St. Michael's Cathedral. "I read about the fire in 1966 and how the townspeople saved the icons," Laurette said.

"They don't have chairs in this church," David told her, still clinging to her hand.

"Are you going to be like some of the tourists and stand in the middle of the road to take a picture?" Diane asked with a smile.

"Think I'll just buy a postcard." Laurette stopped to snap a picture of Katie and David in front of the church.

The walk to the castle was short and the view at the top well worth the climb. When David ran to climb onto a cannon, Laurette called, "Stand on this side of the gun so I can take your picture."

"You handled that well," Diane commented. "Saved me having to holler at him not to climb on it. You're good with children."

I wonder if Ryan likes children. The thought came to Laurette unbidden.

The afternoon went quickly. When dark clouds started to move in, Diane said, "We ought to get back to the office before we get wet."

"Will Daddy be there?" Katie asked.

"I don't know, sweets. He may have been called out to a ship."

"Let's go see." Laurette took the little girl's hand and started down the path.

Drops of rain started to fall before they got back to Southeast Maritime. The children raced up the steps to the second floor. "They should sleep well tonight," Diane quipped.

Squeals of delight echoed back to the women as they started down the hall. Turning into the office, Laurette saw not Tyler but Ryan squatting, with David hanging over one shoulder and Katie on his knee. The look of joy on his face sent a quiver of delight through Laurette. *He does like children.*

When he saw the women, Ryan stood up, taking David's hand and holding Katie in his other arm. "Did you have a nice afternoon?" he asked.

Laurette couldn't speak. Emotion overwhelmed her.

"We got in just ahead of the rain," Diane said, pointing to the window where water cascaded down the pane. "Is Tyler here?"

Ryan's expression became serious. "Afraid not. He had to go to a city council meeting."

"At least he's in town."

His gaze turned to Laurette. "Did you see the sights of Sitka?" he asked quietly.

She nodded, still not trusting her voice.

David wiggled to get free, breaking the spell when Ryan let go of his hand. He gently set Katie on her feet and grabbed David to roughhouse with him.

"The children miss you, Ryan. I wish you would come by the house more often," Diane said.

"You know how summer is," Ryan said, swinging David by his arms. He laughed when the child squealed and begged for more.

This can't be the sullen man who met me at the airport. Laurette marveled at the difference and wondered what was causing it.

"I've got to get these wild ones home," Diane said.

"I'll help you get them in the car," Ryan offered.

His smile sent Laurette's emotions awry. She had difficulty forming the words to thank Diane for such a nice afternoon.

"We'll make a date for you two to come to dinner," Diane offered as she coaxed the children out of the office and down the stairs.

David and Katie went willingly when Ryan scooped one under each arm and carried them down the stairs. They giggled all the way.

Laurette stood mesmerized by this man she thought she knew.

ten

Laurette stood in the doorway listening to the echoes of the happy children. *Is he changing, or am I just getting to know Ryan better? He isn't at all the kind of man I thought he was when I came here.*

Debbie hollered from the other office. "Could you answer the phone for me? I want to clean the coffeepot and wash the cups."

"Sure." Laurette shook away her thoughts of Ryan and went back to work. She picked up a stack of faxes.

"Anything important?"

She looked up at the sound of his voice. "I haven't read them all yet." She perused the rest of the faxes while he hung his wet jacket over the back of a chair. "Nothing urgent," she said when she'd finished.

"You got your rain gear with you?" he asked.

"It's in my truck." She heard the wind howl around the corner of the building. "We were lucky to have the afternoon so clear before this hit."

"You want more coffee?" Debbie asked, coming back with the clean coffeepot and cups. Her expression indicated she hoped his answer was no.

"No thanks. About time to call it a night. We'll take care of those in the morning," Ryan said as Laurette put the fax messages back on the desk.

"I'll walk with you to the parking lot," Debbie said as Laurette pulled on her jacket.

"I'll lock up," Ryan said.

Laurette raced with Debbie from the door of the building

to their parked vehicles. "See you tomorrow," Laurette called, ducking into her truck.

The storm blew all night. Laurette put on her full rain gear before going to work in the morning. As she came through the door of the office, Tyler was putting down a VHF radio. "We've got an injured deckhand coming in."

"What happened?"

"Don't know how, but he has a crushed leg. Coast Guard is on the way with a helicopter to take him to the hospital." He grabbed his coat. "Do you know any nursing?"

"A little first aid," she answered. "Won't there be an EMT on board the helicopter?"

"Probably, but I'm the one who may need the first aid. I can't stand the sight of blood. You'd better come with me."

She clung to the side of the truck as Tyler raced to the Coast Guard station.

"The ambulance will be at the helicopter pad to pick up the injured man."

"You want me to ride with him?"

"I'd appreciate it. Ryan told me how good you were with that heart attack victim that came in earlier this summer."

"I just sat with his wife. Will there be anyone else with this man?"

"Probably not. We'll find out from the ship steward where he's from and notify his family. At least we'll try to. Most of these crews are from foreign countries."

"Will he speak English?" Laurette wondered how she could be of any help to the injured man if she couldn't even communicate with him.

"Most of them do. But I don't think he'll be talking much. With a crushed leg, he'll probably be pretty heavily drugged."

Tyler pulled in next to the ambulance and hopped out to talk to the waiting EMTs. Laurette stood beside him.

Tyler introduced her. "Laurette works for SAM and will be going in the ambulance with the patient."

The young man reached out to shake her hand. "You were there when we took a passenger off a cruise ship a few weeks ago."

She nodded.

"My wife's a nurse; she told me what a good job you did comforting the wife."

Laurette felt her face grow hot. She tried to smile. "Just doing what I could to help."

They all looked up as the chopper roared, settling onto the helipad. The EMTs rushed over with the gurney to get the injured crewman. They covered him with warm blankets and a tarp to keep him dry and warm, then quickly loaded him into the ambulance. Laurette followed and sat next to the unconscious man.

"Please, Lord, comfort and heal this man," she prayed, quietly watching the EMT tend to his IV.

"He's going to need a lot of prayers," the attendant said after adding his amen.

Laurette stayed with the injured deckhand while he was wheeled into the emergency room. Soon he was whisked into an elevator and on his way to the operating room, so Laurette pulled off her rain gear and prepared to wait.

"You plan to stay?" the admitting nurse asked.

"Yes."

"Are you family?"

"No, I'm with Southeast Alaska Maritime. We don't know anything about him yet. I doubt there will be any family close by."

The nurse smiled. "Nice of you to care. Why don't you go to the waiting room and have some coffee. I'll have someone contact you when we know more."

"Okay, thanks." Laurette went to the waiting room and

pulled out her cell phone to call the office.

"Do we have any info yet on the injured deckhand?" she asked when Debbie answered.

"Tyler is on the radio with the ship steward now. Want me to call back when we know his particulars?"

"Yes. The hospital is going to want the information as soon as possible."

"Tyler just said he'll take care of that. Are you coming back to the office?"

"If it's okay with Tyler, I'd like to stay for a while. I want to see how he is and if there's anything I can do."

◆

Laurette poured a cup of coffee and sat down to wait. She had her eyes closed in prayer when a nurse came into the room. "You from Southeast Maritime?"

Laurette sat up quickly. "Yes."

"The man you brought in is in surgery. The leg is pretty mangled, so it may be a few hours. You want me to call your office when he comes out of the OR?"

"If you would, please. I'll come back later so he won't be alone when he finds out what has happened to his leg." Laurette gave the woman her card. "This is my cell phone. Will you let me know so I can be here when he comes to?"

The nurse smiled and put the card in her pocket. "Be glad to."

Laurette called the office. "Hi, Debbie. I need a ride back. Anybody available?"

Twenty minutes later Ryan walked into the waiting room.

Laurette jumped up. "The deckhand will be in surgery for hours, so I can work until I know he's coming out of it."

"Tyler asked you to come back?"

"No. I just don't think the guy should be alone. I plan to sit with him unless Tyler changes his mind about letting me keep the guy company."

Ryan looked puzzled. "Why? They're going to keep him sedated."

"Would you want to wake up alone? Tyler says he's probably from a foreign country, so there won't be any of his family here to comfort him."

Ryan sighed. "You would be the one to think about that." He put his arm around her shoulders. "You're some kind of special."

❧

Laurette's question about being alone haunted Ryan. He saw her leave when the hospital called, and he knew she would sit praying by the stranger's bed for hours. *Who would be there for me?* he wondered. *Mom is in Chicago. I might be just as alone as that poor guy. Would there be a guardian angel to pray for me?*

When the workday came to an end, Ryan went by the fish-and-chips shop to get takeout, then drove to the hospital. He paused at the door of the deckhand's room. Laurette sat, just as he knew she would, at the side of the bed, holding her Bible in her hands and praying quietly while the sedated crewman slept.

"Are you hungry?" he whispered, holding out the boxes of food.

Her smile lit up the room.

"Can you take a break? We can eat in the waiting room down the hall."

She looked at the sleeping patient. "I don't think Joseph will mind."

He guided her to a chair in the waiting room. "Did Tyler find out more than his name? I've been busy and haven't heard much today."

"He's from Italy. His leg is patched up, but he won't be able to go back to the ship for a long time." She took the food Ryan held out. "The cruise line will send him home when he can travel." She took a bite of fish. "This is good. Guess I forgot to eat today. I did remember to call Diane and ask her to make sure Ruth ate something, though."

"How late will you stay here?"

"Not much longer. The nurse says Joseph will sleep for the night. The nurses will call me when he starts waking up—probably sometime tomorrow. I'll come back then."

"So will I," Ryan offered. "And I'm going to add my own prayers for Joseph's recovery to yours." He saw the tears in her eyes and reached to take her hand. "You okay?"

She nodded. "Your prayers will mean a lot to both Joseph and me."

"Hey, you reminded me I could be the one lying there alone."

When they finished eating, Ryan started to pick up the remnants of their supper. "Why don't we go say good night to Joseph and tell him we'll be back tomorrow?"

A few moments later, Ryan walked Laurette to her truck and gently kissed her forehead before she slipped into the vehicle. "See you tomorrow," he said, softly shutting the truck door.

Driving back to his trailer, he thought again how vulnerable he was. As cold and unloving as he'd been to his mother, he wondered if she would even come if he got hurt. He glanced at his watch as he shut the front door behind him. "Too late to call her tonight," he muttered, calculating the three-hour time difference.

He turned on the stereo and plopped down in his chair, Laurette filling his thoughts. *When her job with SAM ends, she'll go back south. I don't have anything to offer her. How could I ask her to stay?*

He could go south and look for a job. He couldn't stand being in an office all day. It would be better to keep doing what he was good at.

On the other hand, if he got a steady job, he could live in a bigger place and have room for a piano. He smiled, trying to picture himself giving kids piano lessons like his mom had.

Can you picture having kids of your own?

Ryan sighed deeply and pulled himself out of the chair. He turned off the stereo and sat down at the organ. The music soothed his troubled mind. Playing the hymns was his way of praying. "If I can follow the notes, maybe I can learn to follow where Jesus leads me."

&

Ryan walked into work late the next morning. Laurette stood with a cup of coffee reading the latest fax. "You oversleep?" she asked with a smile.

"I called my mother," he said quietly. Laurette's look of pleasure warmed his heart. "Must have talked to her for an hour."

She put down her cup and took his hand. "Was she pleased to hear from you?"

He nodded. "I told her about you." He put his hand over hers. "She'd like to meet you."

Laurette looked puzzled.

"I told her you were encouraging me to read the Bible and pray." He squeezed her hands. "She said to tell you how happy she is that I found you."

"And that you found your way back to her."

"Exactly." He didn't voice his feelings about why he was glad he'd found Laurette. He let her hands go. "Have you checked on Joseph?"

"Not yet. I waited to see if you wanted to go with me."

"Let's go."

eleven

When Laurette entered the office the next morning, she saw Ryan pouring coffee. "Want a cup?" he asked.

She nodded. "Any word from the hospital?"

"No." He handed her a cup. "I have to go out with some mail and papers," he said, pointing at a cruise ship in the harbor. "If you're around when I get back, we could run out to see how Joseph is doing today."

"I'd like that. I got some magazines to take him."

Ryan smiled. "It may be awhile before he's alert enough to look at them, but I'm sure the thought will please him." He looked at the clock. "I've got to run."

Laurette watched him pick up a mailbag and some papers and wave as he left. Sighing, she started sorting the faxes that had come in that morning. "I can do this one," she said, pulling out one of the faxes and heading to the post office.

When she returned, Debbie said, "You've got a phone call on line one."

"This is Laurette."

"Laurette, it's John."

"Hello, John. Is Ruth all right?"

"She's fine. It's a nice day, so I'm going to take Mother out for a ride around Sitka. Would you like to join us for a late lunch, say around four o'clock?"

"I'm sorry, John. We have four ships in the harbor today, and I don't think I'll have a spare moment. Thanks for asking me." After chatting a few more moments, she hung up.

"I've got a problem for you," Debbie said. "A passenger

stepped on her glasses and needs them fixed. Can you take care of it?"

"Must be an optometrist in town. Call the ship and make an appointment for which tender she'll be on. I'll get ahold of the optometrist's office and let them know we're coming in." Laurette grabbed the phone book and went to work. It was late afternoon before she and Ryan were both in the office at the same time.

"The last ship will sail at five. Think we can wind things up and go see Joseph?" Ryan asked.

Laurette heaved a sigh. "It's been a wild day, starting with broken glasses and ending with a sprained ankle." She plopped down in a chair. "Yes, I'd like to go see Joseph."

On the way to the hospital, Laurette told Ryan about John's call. "Ruth will be tired and happy tonight. I think I'll just fix her some ice cream or a snack since John was planning on a late lunch." She glanced at her watch. "Probably about now."

"And you think I have bad eating habits." He raised his eyebrows and smiled. "Don't you think we should stop for a bite to eat after we see Joseph?"

"Sounds good. What are you hungry for?"

"How about a hamburger?"

The two entered Joseph's room. The injured crewman's leg hung in a sling, but he could still sit up a little.

"How you doing, Joseph?" Ryan asked jovially.

Joseph appeared groggy but aware that they were not hospital personnel.

"We're from Southeast Alaska Maritime. I'm Laurette, and this is Ryan. I rode in the ambulance with you."

The injured man smiled. "I don't remember much after that rope let go and I got hit."

"Those ropes are huge. The broken end whip around and get you?" Ryan asked.

"Sure did," Joseph mumbled.

"We brought you something to read when you feel better." Laurette laid the magazines on the bedside table.

"Thank you. Someone from your office called. Was it you?" he asked Ryan.

"Must have been our boss, Tyler Healy. Did he let you know the cruise line will take care of you?"

The injured man nodded. "He said he would telegraph my mother."

Laurette stood at the side of the bed. She took the man's work-worn hand in her own. "We're praying for you."

She saw the crewman's eyes fill with tears. "Would you pray for my mother? She depends on the money I send her, and I don't know how long I'll be out of work."

"What's her name?"

"Maria," he whispered as a single tear ran down his weathered cheek.

"We'll pray for both of you," she said, giving his left hand a reassuring squeeze.

Ryan came to her side and shook Joseph's right hand. "We'll check on you again tomorrow. You let our office know if there is anything we can do for you."

"Thanks," he murmured.

Walking back to the car, Ryan took Laurette's hand. "You're good with people. You made that guy feel better."

"I hope so. All I offered was to pray for him."

"I saw his tears. You touched him with your kindness." He opened the car door for her but gave her a quick hug before letting her get in. "You touch a lot of us in special ways," he said softly.

Ryan started the car and headed for the restaurant, and Laurette tried to calm her runaway pulse. *Is it his touch or his words that make me tingle clear to my toes?*

Settled over hamburgers, Ryan asked, "You got plans for

when you go back to Seattle?"

"Not really. I don't think I want to go for any more education. Costs too much and I'm tired of school."

"So what are you going to do?"

She put the half-eaten sandwich on her plate and looked at him. "I don't know what to do. Guess I'll have to find a job."

He looked into her brown eyes and saw the flecks of gold. "What kind of job?"

She sighed. "My degree is in biology. Mostly I worked with plants, so I guess I could find a job in a greenhouse or nursery."

He took her hands in his. "You have a gift—you're very good with people. They need you a lot more than some potted plants do."

She rewarded him with a smile. "And you have the gift of music. What are you going to do?" She pulled back her hands and picked up her sandwich.

Find a way to be near you. Aloud he said, "I don't know."

Ryan took Laurette back to the parking lot and her truck. She slipped out of his car. "Thanks for dinner. I'll see you in the morning." And she was gone.

I can't let her go. I've got to find a better job so I have something to offer her. Ryan was free to come into the Dockside Hotel lounge whenever he wanted. He went there now to play the piano and to try to think.

❧

Laurette drove home in deep thought. *What am I going to do? I studied biology thinking I could help on the farm. My brother will run the farm, and I don't think I want to marry a farmer. So what do I do with my education?*

She found Ruth sleeping in her chair. Her old friend roused with a beautiful smile. "Is it morning already?"

Laurette kissed Ruth's cheek. "No. You were just having a little nap in your chair. Now tell me about your day with John."

Ruth's glowing face and stories of driving along the water-front pushed back Laurette's worries of her own future.

"We went by the Pioneer Home. Esther lived there and I used to go visit her."

"Is it a nice place?"

"Oh, yes. It's just for Native Alaskans. Esther always said the people living there had interesting stories to tell. Sometimes she would share them with me."

"Did you have a nice lunch?"

"Yes. I won't need anything else to eat tonight, but you should fix yourself something."

"Ryan and I stopped for a hamburger, so I'm not hungry, either. Later on we could have some ice cream. Would you like to have me read the Bible now?"

"Yes, please."

Ruth's stories of her day out continued for a week. Usually Ruth thought it had happened yesterday or occasionally in the distant past. On Sunday Laurette shared stories of Ruth's outing with Diane.

"Why don't you try to take her out more often? Take her to Sheet'ka Kwaan Naa Kahidi. She'd love it."

"I beg your pardon? I can't even say it," Laurette protested.

Diane laughed. "It's a longhouse built in the traditional Nakaahidi design to preserve the Tlingit culture. They have storytelling and dance performances. Ruth would love it."

"Where is it?"

"Down on Katlian Street, close to where you live."

"I'll do it the next time I can get away for a couple hours."

An opportunity presented itself the following week. Ruth did enjoy seeing the longhouse. People there seemed to know her and showed her where some of her late sister Esther's baskets were displayed.

Ryan met them when they got home. He had come by to barbecue salmon. They enjoyed a fine meal together.

"You come rest, Ruth. I'll help Rette with the dishes," Ryan offered.

That evening Ruth regaled them with stories of her sister's beadwork and baskets. "She did beautiful work," she said with a deep sigh.

"The ones we saw today were very nice. Did you make baskets, too?" Laurette asked.

"Not the perfect ones like Esther. She's the artist in the family. I miss her so."

The excitement had tired Ruth, so she kept the evening devotions short. Ryan stood when she pushed herself up out of her chair. She reached up to pat his cheek. "You did a good job on the salmon."

He gave her a hug as Ruth bade them good night and went to her room.

"She did well today," Laurette said, putting her Bible away. "Everyone was so kind to her. Even when she kept forgetting their names."

"Must be hard for her here alone day after day. We should try to get her out more often."

"I worry about how much longer she can stay alone."

"You're here for her now. She'll be okay for a while, but she sure will miss you when you go back to Seattle." Ryan brushed the stray curls back from her forehead.

Laurette couldn't read the look in his eyes. "I'm going to miss a lot of things about Sitka," she murmured.

Ryan stood up. "I should get going."

She walked him to the door. His kiss started softly and quickly intensified, causing her to lose all sense of reality. She felt like she was floating off into the clouds.

He broke away after a gentle hug. "See you in the morning." And he was gone.

Laurette stared at the empty driveway before finally going back into the house and preparing for bed.

His kiss lingered in her memory. Even when they were busy in the office, just being near Ryan left her with a flush of happiness.

"Got time to stop for supper tonight?" he asked a few days later.

"I need to get home to Ruth."

"She doesn't watch the clock," he reminded her.

"You're right. I can come in an hour late. Want to grab some fish-and-chips?"

"You're as addicted to fish-and-chips as I am to chocolate milk."

"They don't have fish this good where I grew up." She poked his arm on their way to the parking lot.

They enjoyed their supper, and Laurette ordered a take-out meal for Ruth. When they got back outside, she reached over to give Ryan a quick kiss on the cheek and ran for her truck.

❧

The house was quiet when she entered. "Ruth, are you sleeping? I've brought you some fish-and-chips."

There was no answer. Laurette went into the living room, then hurried into Ruth's bedroom and all through the house. "Ruth? Ruth, where are you?" she called frantically.

Grabbing the phone in the living room, she called Ryan at home. While it rang she prayed. *Please, Jesus, let him be home.*

"Hello."

"Ryan, I need you. Ruth has disappeared."

"Is she with John?"

"He's out fishing, and her friends always leave me a note if they take her out. I don't know where she is."

"I'll be right there."

twelve

Laurette grabbed the phone directory. First she called Ruth's church. She got the office recorder. Desperate, she called John's cell phone. She got the "out of service" message. She put the phone down and paced the living room. Where could Ruth have gone?

Racing through the house again, Laurette checked and found Ruth's jacket gone. Her pocketbook that usually sat on her dresser was also gone.

When she heard tires crunching on the driveway gravel, she ran to the door. Ryan jumped out of the car almost before it stopped. He pulled her into his arms. "Now tell me what happened."

"I came home and found the house empty. I've looked and looked, but there's no note. Her coat and purse are both gone, so I know she's gone out."

He smoothed her hair. "Let's assume she took a walk and got lost. We'll go down the hill to the street and starting asking people if they've seen her. Do you have a picture of Ruth?"

His quiet voice calmed Laurette's fears. "I've got a snapshot I took a few weeks ago." She quickly turned to find the picture.

"We'll take my car." He touched her cheek tenderly. "We couldn't get the three of us in your truck."

"Thanks. I'm so worried I don't think I should be driving, anyway." Laurette slid into the passenger seat. She pressed her nose against the window trying to search the side of the road as Ryan drove down the hill to Katlian Street. "Where do we start?" Her heart stayed in her throat, making it hard to speak.

"I'll park here and we'll go down one way and back the other."

"Should we call the police?"

"Wouldn't hurt."

Laurette pulled out her cell phone. The officer who answered told her they couldn't take an official missing person report this soon. When she said it was Ruth, he told Laurette, "I know John Stevenson. I'll send word out for the policemen on duty to be looking for his mother. Will you please keep us informed?"

Shutting the phone, Laurette relayed the message to Ryan. "Here." She handed him Ruth's picture. "Could you do the talking?"

As they walked the nearly deserted street, Laurette peered into the shop windows. It was after seven in the evening, and nothing was open. The farther they went, the more guilt plagued her. *I shouldn't have stopped for dinner on the way home without calling to see if Ruth was okay first. Where has she gone?*

They had walked all the way to the Pioneer Home. "Maybe she came here looking for Esther." Laurette pushed open the door.

"We haven't seen Mrs. Stevenson today," the receptionist told the couple. "Her son brought her by a week or so ago, but she hasn't been back."

"Let's turn around and check the other side of the street." Ryan took Laurette's arm as they started back toward the car.

≈

Ryan stepped in front of her and took hold of her shoulders.

He looked into Rette's fear-glazed eyes. He took her chin and raised her face so she had to look directly at him. "You told me that we have to let go. We have to let the Lord take over," he said sternly. He watched her swallow. A faint smile curved her lips.

"You're telling me to have faith?"

"I am repeating what you told me. Now can we say a prayer and put Ruth in the Lord's hands?" He let his hands drop from her shoulders.

She nodded faintly.

Ryan had never felt so protective of someone. And he had never seen Rette like this. She had always been in total control. In the moment he knew she could be soft and vulnerable, he knew he loved her even more. He wanted to take care of her forever.

Laurette took his hands. "Can you say a prayer for us to find Ruth?"

He squeezed her hands and prayed, "Dear Lord, we put Ruth in Your hands. If it is Your will, guide us to her. Amen."

"Amen," Laurette whispered.

Ryan turned and saw a man walking toward them. "Pardon me, but have you seen this woman? She's lost." He held the snapshot out to the stranger.

"I think she's the one in the P Bar. Looked like she was sleeping off too much to drink."

Ryan still held one of Laurette's hands and gripped her tighter. "Thank you, sir. We'll go check it out."

"Ruth in a bar. What's a pea bar?"

Ryan smiled. "It's been here forever. It's the Pioneer Bar, but the sailors call it the P Bar. It's not far from here. Let's go."

Neon lights reflected on the sidewalk, and noise poured out the door. Ryan gave Laurette an encouraging hug as she moved ahead of him into the tavern. They peered through the smoky haze but saw no one resembling Ruth. They'd turned to approach the bartender with Ruth's photograph when Ryan suddenly spotted a back booth that looked empty. Two men had started toward it, then turned and took a vacant table instead. He nudged Laurette toward the booth. As they got closer, they saw the top of a gray head just below the back of the seat.

"Ruth," Laurette gasped. She slid into the booth next to her friend. Ruth's chin had rested on her chest as she dozed. Now she sat up with a start.

"Oh, Ruth, I thought you were lost." Laurette put her arm around the woman's shoulders. "How did you get here?"

Ryan had slipped into the other side of the booth. Ruth's eyes looked glazed. He saw the concern in Rette's face and longed to comfort both women.

"You know this little lady?" a waiter asked.

"Yes," Laurette and Ryan spoke at once.

"We saw her walking up and down the street. She looked lost and cold, so we brought her inside for some hot tea. Your friend couldn't seem to remember where she lived or tell us who we should call. I asked if she had any ID, and she said she couldn't find any in her purse." He wiped his hands on his apron. "My boss thought someone would come looking for her. Glad to see he was right."

"Has she been here long?" Ryan asked.

The waiter looked at the clock. "Got busy in here and we kind of forgot, I guess. Must be a couple hours." A sheepish grin spread across his face.

"Thank you for looking out for her." Laurette smiled at the man, her arm still wrapped around Ruth. "Where were you going today?"

"I came to find Esther. We go to the antique shops around here." She looked puzzled. "They weren't open and Esther didn't come."

Ryan reached across the table and took the woman's wrinkled hand. "It's late, Ruth. The shops are closed for the night. It's time to go home now." He then spoke to Rette. "I'll go get the car and pull up out front."

She nodded as he got out of the booth.

Ryan pulled a couple of bills out of his pocket and gave them to the waiter on the way out. "Thanks for taking care of her."

"Is she your grandmother?"

"She's a dear friend," Ryan said, then headed for his car.

When they got Ruth home, Laurette helped her get ready for bed. Ryan started the teakettle, but Ruth was too tired to eat or drink. He had the teapot on the table when Rette came back from tucking Ruth in.

"Sit down and relax. It's over."

"I have to call the police back." He watched as she sat down and pulled out the cell phone. When she hung up, she said, "The officer told me to have John come in and register his mother. If this happens again and anyone calls, the police will know who she is. He also said we should get an ID bracelet for her to wear with her name and address, who to call, and all that."

Ryan poured her a cup of tea. "What will happen to her when you move back to Seattle?"

"I don't want to think about it." Rette sipped her tea. "It will be hard to leave here," she whispered, putting the cup down. Ryan felt like he could drown in the depth of her eyes when she looked up at him. Could he be part of the reason she didn't want to leave Sitka?

"You should stay with her tomorrow. This outing has probably been quite a trauma for her, and she shouldn't be left alone after this. At least not until you've told John." Ryan carried the cups to the sink.

Laurette followed him to the door and put her arms around his waist. "I don't know what I would have done without you tonight." She pressed her face against his chest, and he pulled her into his embrace.

"You always try to take care of others. I'm glad I could help this time."

She looked up with tears in her eyes. He gently kissed her forehead. *I always want to be there to help.* His hands slid up to tangle in her curly hair. Ryan slowly tipped her head farther back so he could kiss her lips, then released her and whispered, "Call me anytime." He touched her face one more time before he went out the door.

❧

Laurette stood in the doorway. She waved as he got in his car and drove away. Tears streamed down her face. *I feel so safe in his arms.*

Absently she went back to the kitchen to rinse out the cups. She checked on Ruth and found her old friend sleeping soundly.

Sleep wouldn't come for Laurette, so she took out her laptop and wrote to her mother about Ruth getting lost. She explained how much help Ryan had been in finding her. She admitted to her mother that Ryan had become more than a friend. *"I don't know what I'm going to do,"* she confessed to her mother. She read the message over but decided not to send it yet. "I'm not ready to share my confusion—not even with my mother," she murmured.

Laurette spent a restless night. Several times she got up to check on Ruth, who slept peacefully. When her housemate woke at nine, Laurette had been up for hours. She had cleaned the bathroom and kitchen and done all the laundry. She had called Ryan and assured him she would come in as soon as she knew Ruth would be all right. Next she called Ruth's pastor.

"John has talked to me about his mother," the vicar said. "He tells me what a wonderful job you do taking care of her, and he knows you must leave when your job ends. We are all grateful to you for helping Ruth stay in her home a while longer. We also know the time will come when she will need more care. I'll talk to the pastoral care committee and have them call morning and afternoon to check on Ruth. If there are times when you want to be away, let us know and we will be there for Ruth. We'll keep you and Ruth in our prayers."

Laurette thanked the man and hung up. She had written down his private number in case she needed him when the church office was closed.

"Oh, you're home." Ruth came into the kitchen wrapped in her robe. "I was just going to make a cup of tea."

"Are you hungry? I could scramble some eggs and make toast while you make us some tea."

"That sounds good." Ruth put the teakettle on to boil, hummed happily while she set the table, then sat down, but she looked puzzled.

"Why are you home? Do you have a day off?"

"I stayed to make sure you were all right. Do you remember going for a walk yesterday?"

Ruth nodded. "I got confused and couldn't remember where I was." She looked up with a radiant smile. "But you came and got me."

"You scared me, Ruth. I didn't know where you were. Please don't go out alone anymore. I'll take you anyplace you want to go."

"You are so sweet. You shouldn't worry so much." She looked at the plate of breakfast Laurette put in front of her. "It's wonderful having you here, and you're such a good cook, too." Ruth smiled and picked up her fork.

thirteen

The weather stayed clear. Ruth stayed home.

"Does she remember being lost?" Ryan asked a few days later.

"Yes, but she doesn't seem concerned, because we found her. Who knows how long she slept in that booth. She may think it was only a matter of minutes." She took the coffee Ryan had poured for her. "John is due back anytime. I don't know what he'll do."

"You don't think he would be angry with you, do you? You're there for Ruth every day."

She shook her head. "It's not that. My thoughts are selfish." She sipped the coffee. "If John puts her in the Pioneer Home, I won't have a place to live."

"Oh, I hadn't thought of that." Ryan turned as Debbie called him to the phone.

They didn't have time to talk about personal problems again that day. When Laurette got ready to leave for the night, Ryan still had not come back to the office.

"He had to take a harbor pilot off a cruise ship with the company boat. Said he'd be back late," Debbie told her. "Tyler's been called up to Hyder to load a log ship again. It's just you and me. Let's go home." She pushed the button to put the phone on record.

❧

John's truck was in the driveway when she parked. "Good, I need to talk to him."

"Smells good in here," she called, entering the kitchen.

John came from the living room. "Came home with a

100

boatload of sockeye salmon. Thought we'd have some for supper."

"What can I do to help?"

"Would you set the table?"

"John, I need to talk to you," she said quietly as she took plates from the cupboard. She told him about Ruth getting lost, then said, "The police want you to register her with them. If she wanders off again, they can officially start looking right away instead of having to wait as though she were a missing person."

John looked stricken. "I knew it was coming, but she seems so good when I'm here. I do appreciate all you've done for Mom. She would have had to go into the Pioneer Home by now without you living here."

Laurette longed to know if he would make that decision now but didn't ask. "I took the liberty of ordering an ID bracelet for her. It has her name, address, phone, and your cell phone number—and the pastor of her church suggested including his private phone number, too. If it happens again, whoever finds her will be able to contact someone to come get her."

"Thank you, Laurette. Did Mom say why she went out alone?"

"She went to find Esther so they could go shopping together. It's so sad that she sometimes forgets her sister passed away." Laurette's heart ached with pity. "We have no idea how long she walked up and down the street. The waiter in the bar said she had been there for possibly two hours."

John rubbed his hands together and sighed deeply. "Do you think she understands she isn't to go out alone anymore?"

"Yes, I think she does. But I don't know if she'll always remember that. People from her church are calling her in the morning and afternoon now, just in case. They probably interrupt her afternoon nap, but at least we know where she is."

"What are you two doing in the kitchen? Did you burn the fish, John?" Ruth called from the living room.

"Supper is almost ready, Mother. Would you like to come to the table now?" He looked at Laurette. "We'll talk more later."

⁊⦿

By morning, the sunshine had disappeared into a heavy mist. Tyler looked up when Laurette came into the office.

"How was Hyder?"

"Glad I got back last night. No planes will land in Sitka today."

Ryan had come in after Laurette and heard this last declaration. "An entertainer was due on the noon flight. We're supposed to get her to the cruise ship leaving this afternoon."

"What's their route? Are they going up the Neva Straits?" Tyler asked.

Ryan nodded and grabbed a tide table. "High tide is at three ten; the captain's going to have to sail two o'clock."

Laurette looked from one to the other. It was a narrow strait, and the ships could only make it through on a high tide. The scenery left the passengers breathless, so the cruise lines made the passage as often as they could.

"Could we get the entertainer on an earlier flight?" Laurette asked.

"Won't help if she can't land here," Ryan said.

"But if she gets into Juneau earlier, she'll be ready to hop a flight back here as soon as the fog clears."

"It's a thought. I'll see what I can do." Tyler picked up the phone.

She and Ryan started on the daily routine of taking care of cruise ship requests. The fog remained solid, and the noon flight went north without stopping. By one o'clock, the fog and mist had started to break up.

Laurette stopped by the office to check in. "Got time to

grab a sandwich?" she asked Ryan, who had followed her up the stairs.

They turned as Tyler hung up the phone. "That was our entertainer. She's on the two fifteen flight from Juneau."

Laurette looked at Ryan but did not voice her question.

"Can you do it?" Tyler asked Ryan.

"I think so. The water isn't too choppy."

"Take Laurette with you. She can keep the woman calm."

"Let's go." Ryan patted her on the back as he went by.

"What are we going to do?" Laurette asked, trying to keep up with Ryan's long stride.

He grinned. "We can grab take-out sandwiches on our way to the airport."

"Somehow I don't think that's the whole story." She hopped in the company van. "Then what do we do?"

"We transport the entertainer and her luggage to her ship before it gets to the straits."

"By boat?" She gasped.

He nodded, pulling up to the drive-in. "What do you want for lunch?"

"I seem to have lost my appetite," she muttered.

He grinned at her and ordered them each a sandwich, with a soda for her and chocolate milk for him. "You'd better keep up your strength. I'm going to need your help."

৶

Ryan pulled out a sign just like the one he had held up for Laurette some months ago. Only the name had been changed. An attractive young woman approached them.

"Are you from Southeast Alaska Maritime? I was told they would meet me."

"Yes, Miss Thomas. I'm Ryan and this is Laurette. We're going to take you to your ship," Ryan told her. "Our time is short, so please point out your luggage as soon as it comes out." He hurried her to the baggage carousel.

Miss Thomas pointed to a large suitcase marked HEAVY. "There's one more small one. I have to carry costumes, so I need the big case," she apologized.

Ryan flipped the van keys to Laurette. "Why don't you pull up by the front door? It'll save us a few minutes."

A minute later, after Ryan hurriedly pulled the small suitcase from the carousel, Miss Thomas asked, "Is there a problem with time? When does the ship sail?" She struggled to keep up with Ryan.

He sighed. "This is going to be a rough trip. The ship sailed at two to make the tide. We're going to take you to it by boat."

"Why didn't they wait for me?" she asked indignantly as they reached the place where Laurette had parked the van.

"The ships have to go through the straits at high tide. They didn't have any choice," Ryan explained as he stowed her bags in the back of the van. "Do you have some tennis shoes or something more practical than those?" He pointed to her high heels.

He thanked Laurette as she handed him the keys and got in the backseat.

"I knew I shouldn't have taken this gig," Miss Thomas muttered. "I have some running shoes in my small bag."

"You can change while we get your gear loaded into the boat," Laurette suggested. "If you can, it would be wise to change into jeans and a sweatshirt, too. That looks like an expensive suit."

Ryan noted the fear in his passenger's face as he raced to Crescent Harbor. "We'll take good care of you," he said, trying to reassure the entertainer.

She smiled weakly. "Mother told me to be a teacher."

Ryan left the women to find proper attire while he loaded the large suitcase. "Must weigh a hundred pounds," he muttered, stowing it in the bow of the boat. "Wonder what those costumes are made of."

Laurette handed him the smaller case, then helped Miss Thomas into the boat and guided her to the passenger seat facing the bow. She took the bench that shared the seat back of the forward-facing passenger spot.

Ryan took the boat out of the harbor. As soon as he passed the No Wake Zone, he opened the throttle up. "Hang on," he called to the women. "A little choppy out here." Glancing at Miss Thomas, he noted her white face and grim look. Laurette looked like she was having fun as the boat pounded over the waves. He noted that she had wisely put on her rain gear so the spray coming over the side of the speeding boat didn't soak her.

"Rette, will you take the wheel?" he yelled. "Just like driving a car, only the road is bigger," he teased as she slid behind the wheel. He stood in the opening in the canvas where he had a better view. "Head for that point. Don't touch the throttle unless I tell you, understood?"

Laurette nodded as she stood next to him. He glowed with pride at how quickly she learned to stand while holding the wheel to keep the boat going where he indicated. "You're doing great." He wanted to put his arm around her but didn't think it proper while they had a passenger.

He turned to Miss Thomas. "You okay?"

She nodded, her knuckles white from gripping the bar in front of her.

"There, I think I see the ship," Laurette shouted.

"Looks like it. Head right for it. I'll take over when we get close," Ryan told her.

He squatted down where he could talk to the entertainer. "I told you this would be a tough one. We'll come up alongside the ship, then hold the same speed while we transfer you and your luggage aboard."

"Will they open a door for me?" Her eyes were as big as saucers.

"It will be above the water level. The crew will help you aboard." Before she could question him further, he grabbed the VHF radio to talk to the ship.

"Thanks, Rette. You did a great job," Ryan said when he took over the wheel. "Can you help Miss Thomas get ready?"

He saw Laurette kneel next to the frightened woman to talk to her. He concentrated on bringing the boat alongside the cruise ship. He waved to the sailors who had opened the deck door several feet above them. Within a couple minutes, he'd matched their speed and was holding steady directly under the opening. He signaled to the sailors.

"Rette, I need you to take the wheel a minute. I'll get Miss Thomas's luggage loaded."

"You can do it," he whispered as she slid into the seat behind the wheel. "Don't look at the water. Just hold us steady under that opening." He pointed to the side of the ship.

He grabbed the heavy rope net the sailors tossed down, loaded the luggage into it, and signaled for the men to pull it aboard.

Miss Thomas had moved to the stern to watch the process. "Will they pull me up like that?" Her voice trembled.

He stood up and watched the luggage inch its way up the side of the moving ship. "Not exactly. They'll give you a ladder to climb." He smiled at her. "Just think of it as a new part of your act."

"I should have listened to my mother," she groaned.

Ryan checked on Laurette. She kept her eyes on the open deck above them and held the boat close to the ship. *That's my girl.* The ladder fell into the back of the boat, breaking into his thoughts of Laurette. "Are you ready for this?" Ryan asked the entertainer.

Miss Thomas shuddered. He saw her press her lips together and held the ladder while she put a foot on the first rung. "Take it slow. I'll hold the ladder as steady as I can.

Now go." He gave her boost up and held her legs as long as he could reach. She only had a few more rungs to go when the sailors at the top took her hands and pulled her aboard.

A cheer went up. Miss Thomas stood and bravely waved to Ryan.

He gave her a thumbs-up and moved to take the wheel from Laurette.

She heaved a sigh of relief and slid to the passenger seat.

Ryan turned them away from the ship and headed back to Sitka at a slower speed. "You did a perfect job." He smiled. "Were you praying the whole time?"

"I've never prayed so hard in my life. What if that poor woman had fallen?"

"I bet she goes home after this and becomes a teacher." He reached to take her hand. "I prayed for her, too. Thank God our prayers were answered so quickly and so perfectly."

fourteen

The hectic pace of work kept Laurette's mind off her personal problems. At times the thoughts of what she would do if Ruth had to go into assisted living jumped out to worry her. John remained attentive, but she knew he wanted to get back out to fish while the sockeye were still running. The canneries paid him a good price for the red salmon. He had registered Ruth with the police, but her ID bracelet still had not arrived. *Just trust God to take care of her,* Laurette reminded herself as she climbed the stairs to the office.

"Your father ever shoot skeet?" Tyler asked as she came through the door.

She shook her head. "He didn't keep guns around the house. Said he didn't have time to hunt." She grinned. "Besides, the pheasants and ducks were my mother's pets. I'm not sure what she would have done if he or Brian ever shot any. I know she wouldn't have cooked them." She picked up the fax messages. "You going hunting?"

"No, but we just got a request for clay pigeons. A cruise director wants to have people shoot skeet off the back deck. Seems the ones he had shipped for that purpose got broken, and he needs us to replace them."

"They sure request some interesting stuff." Laurette looked up as Ryan walked in.

"What now?" he asked.

Tyler explained the problem.

"What about the gun club? I think they have skeet shoots sometimes."

Tyler raised his eyebrows. "Never heard of one here, but

that's a good idea. Will you find out who runs it and give them a call?"

"Sure. How soon do we need the clay pigeons, and how many do they want?" Ryan asked.

"Here's the fax." Laurette handed him a sheet from the ones she had been reading. "I'll take care of this one. A woman needs to go to the dentist."

Tyler got up and grabbed his jacket and pointed out the window toward the huge ship in the harbor. "I've got to put a harbor pilot aboard." Laurette had started out the door when he called, "Diane wants you to call when you get a chance."

Laurette waved and headed for the dock to pick up the passenger needing dental attention.

ॐ

Ryan sat down in Tyler's seat and started calling people about the clay pigeons.

"Yeah, I got a couple cases I can spare. They're at the clubhouse," the manager told Ryan. "I'm on my way out now. Could you pick them up after four?"

After making an appointment with the man, Ryan put the phone down and wondered if Laurette would like to go along. He hadn't had time to ask about Ruth for a couple of days, and it would give them a chance to talk.

What will you do when Rette leaves? If Ruth goes into the nursing home, she'll have to find a new place to live. Or would she quit SAM early and go back to Seattle?

I've got to find time to look for a year-round job. I have to have something to offer her before I can ask her to stay in Sitka. Ryan pushed aside his worrisome thoughts and went back to solving problems for the cruise ships in the harbor.

ॐ

While Laurette waited to take the passenger at the dentist back to the dock, she called Diane.

"Have you ever seen the Russian Dancers?" her friend asked.

"No. Never have time when they have a show."

"You know they're housewives who perform authentic Russian dances. Their costumes alone are worth seeing."

"I hear the passengers off the ships talk about them. I'll go see them before the summer's over."

"That's why I wanted to talk to you. My neighbor is one of the dancers, and she's given me tickets. I checked the schedule, and you only have two ships on Thursday. Will you go with me?"

"Have to check with the boss, but since it's you asking, I think he'll let me off early."

❧

On Thursday when Laurette ran into the restaurant a bit late, she stopped still. "Ruth, how nice to see you." She looked at Diane. "You didn't tell me Ruth could go, too."

Diane patted Ruth's hand. "It's our surprise."

Ruth beamed. Laurette gave her a kiss on the cheek and pulled her chair close to her old friend.

"I let the church know so no one will worry when they call this afternoon and Ruth isn't there to answer."

"You thought of everything."

They enjoyed lunch, then went to the Centennial Building. "I was here for the music festival, but the curtains behind the stage were open then," Laurette commented.

"The dark background will make the costumes stand out better," Diane explained.

An hour later, when they came out of the show, Diane asked Ruth if she would like to take the long way home.

The old woman's eyes sparkled. "I'd like that. I still love sightseeing, even after all these years."

Laurette smiled and helped Ruth into Diane's car. "I went out to the gun club with Ryan the other night, and he took me up to Harbor Mountain. What a view. We could see all of Sitka Sound."

"You sound like a tourist," Diane teased. "Enjoy it while you can. The wet, dreary winter will be here soon enough."

"I guess I'll be back in rainy Seattle by then," Laurette said sadly.

"I don't like to think of you going away," Ruth said quietly. "I never get to see my grandchildren—haven't since they left Sitka. Will you ever come back?"

"I'm not sure I want to leave," Laurette admitted with a sigh.

Diane drove to Katlian Street and parked near Totem Square. "Are you up to walking a little?" she asked Ruth.

Ruth seemed happy to walk between the two young women. "When Esther lived there," she said as she pointed across the street to the Pioneer Home, "we used to come over here and try to figure out what the totem meant." She chuckled. "My sister would make up silly stories about it. She said those old petroglyphs looked like something I had drawn."

Laurette hugged Ruth. "You must miss your sister a lot."

"Yes, but soon we'll be together again."

"I hope not for a while. We aren't ready to let you go," Laurette protested.

"The Lord will decide," Ruth said, stopping to catch her breath.

"We should get you home before you wear us all out, Ruth," Diane said. Ruth smiled at Diane's teasing, then they all turned back toward the car. "I'll drop you off and then take Laurette back to her truck."

❧

"Thanks for taking us sightseeing, Diane," Laurette said.

"I just hope Ruth doesn't get the idea to go on her own," Diane said, turning back toward the office.

"Me, too." Laurette heaved a big sigh. "She is so sweet, and I don't want anything to happen to her." She added wistfully, "I don't want to leave her."

"I keep telling you to stay in Sitka. One of our winters will cure you of thinking Seattle is a rainy place."

"I may have to go back to Seattle sooner if John decides to put Ruth in the Pioneer Home. I won't have a place to live."

"Wouldn't he let you continue to live in her house?"

"Why? Don't you think he'll want to sell it or even move there himself?"

"Well, if you need a place to stay, the kids can share a room and you can come live with us." Diane pulled in behind Laurette's truck. "There's no reason to make a rushed decision."

"Thanks. I would like to finish my job here, and I don't want to go back to the B and B. It's just too expensive, long-term. I've looked in the paper and haven't found anything else available yet."

Diane reached over to pat Laurette's hand. "The Lord has a plan. We just have to be patient until He tells us what it is."

As Diane drove away, Laurette decided not to get in her truck. Ruth would be asleep, so she would just stop by the office for a minute to see what was going on. She climbed the stairs.

The look of pleasure on Ryan's face when he saw her made her heart skip a beat. "Thought you'd gone with Diane."

"I did. She just dropped me off to pick up my truck, and I came in to check on you."

"You don't think I can handle this alone?" he quipped.

Laurette felt her face grow hot. "I didn't mean to criticize. You do great." She looked at the clock. "But you're working late. Problems?"

"No. Tyler got called to Ketchikan, so I'm double-checking what has to be done tomorrow."

"Need help?"

"I will tomorrow." He waved the stack of faxes. "Always something to handle." He leaned back in his chair. "I've been meaning to ask you about Ruth. Is she staying home?"

"No, we—" Before she could continue, Ryan leaned forward in his chair.

"Did she take off again?"

"Relax." She put her hands up as if to push him back in the chair. "Diane took Ruth and me to see the Russian Dancers. Then we walked through Totem Square. Maybe if we take her out often enough, she won't feel like going for a walk alone."

"What's John planning to do about her situation?"

"He had to go back out fishing. He needs to get another haul of sockeye. We agreed that with the extra people keeping tabs on Ruth, she's fine at home for now. And he insists that I don't have to feel bad if something else happens since I'm not technically her caregiver, but it's hard not to feel responsible for her."

"I'd tell you to quit worrying, but now I'm doing it. Given any more thought to what you'll do if Ruth goes in the nursing home before fall?"

"Diane offered to let me live there if I can't find another place to stay." She looked at him and felt her face flush. "I–I don't want to leave until my job is over," she stammered. *I don't want to leave you.*

"I don't want you to go, either." His voice sounded husky. Then he grinned. "We need you to keep running people to the medical clinic and holding their hands when they're sick."

"I should get home. Need to get my rest if I'm to keep working." She smiled. "It is nice to know I'm needed."

"Hey, let's check the schedule and plan another fishing trip. Can you get away? Or do you feel you should stay home with Ruth?"

"Her church will have someone there whenever I want to go out."

"Wednesday next week looks good. The last ship sails at two, so we should be out of here shortly after noon."

"I'll bring the lunch. Can you guarantee me good weather and lots of fish?"

"You sound like a tourist."

"I feel like one with all the sightseeing I've been doing. Now I'm off to check on my roommate." She waved as she went out the door.

fifteen

Wednesday dawned bright and clear. Laurette had filled her day pack with a heavy sweatshirt and fleece vest Tuesday night. She always kept her rain gear handy. This morning she packed a small cooler with ham sandwiches, cookies, and apples. Ryan would bring chips and soda. She looked around the kitchen before leaving for work. Emmy and Mike Littlefield were going to take Ruth to their home for the day. Mike would take the last pilot off a ship early in the afternoon and be back to spend time with the ladies. Laurette smiled thinking of Mike. He always asked if the truck he'd sold her needed any repairs.

Pulling into the parking lot at work, Laurette noticed that Ryan had his boat and trailer waiting to be launched. *He and Tyler must have traded vehicles last night,* she thought, bounding up the stairs to start her day with SAM.

"You look bright and cheerful as usual," Tyler greeted her. "Ready to catch lots of fish?"

"I'm ready to go fishing. Catching is a bonus."

"Ryan's picking up some freight at the airport. I'll be around so hopefully you two can get an early start."

"Sounds good. What needs to be done?" She glanced at the messages on his desk.

By noon they had cleared up most of the work to be done. "Debbie and I can handle what's left. You two take a deserved day off," Tyler instructed.

Ryan smiled at Laurette, sending her heart into a tailspin. "Let's go," he said softly.

She climbed on the trailer hitch to put her pack and

cooler in the boat before Ryan backed it down the ramp. "Remember what to do?" he asked.

She nodded and gripped the bow rope. As soon as the boat floated free of the trailer, she maneuvered it to the dock and held it there until Ryan parked the trailer and joined her. An eagle called. She loved the sound and tried to spot where the bird perched.

Ryan pointed to a tree on the beach. "Look for the white head against the green."

"Oh, I see it." She turned to him in awe. "They are so majestic."

As they left the harbor, Laurette breathed in the salt air. The deep blue sky was reflected in a calm sea, the sun making it look like a giant mirror. She closed her eyes and thanked God for the beauty that surrounded them.

When Ryan took the boat past Mitchell Rock, Laurette stood next to him to look over the windshield. As the boat gained speed, the wind washed over her face. She pulled off her hat so it wouldn't blow away, and the breeze ruffled her hair. Standing close to Ryan in this majestic scene sent a shiver of delight down her spine.

"It's so calm; let's go across. We can look around St. Lazeria Island. Should have come out in May and June. That's when the birds are nesting."

"Is that Bird Island? They don't let people go ashore, do they?"

"Yes, it's one of the largest seabird colonies in southeast Alaska. Wildlife people don't like anyone walking around the island. Could damage the nesting areas. We'll just cruise around."

"Okay. Look, there's the Fuji look-alike again. When are we going to climb it?" She pointed to their right at the snowcapped mountain silhouetted against the blue sky. Small puffy white clouds floated above Mt. Edgecumbe.

He gave her a dazzling smile. "We'll find time. You seem to attract good weather when we go sightseeing."

She drank in the beauty of the water and approaching islands. *I never want to leave here,* she thought. Ryan's arm brushed against her. *I never want to leave him,* her conscience insisted.

Ryan throttled down as they drew close to St. Lazaria. "We'll coast in slow. Something like eleven different species live here. A bird-watcher's dream come true."

Laurette looked at the rugged coastline. "I don't think I'd like to land there. Too many rocks."

"See those dark shadows?" Ryan nosed the boat toward them. "They're caves. I'll go near enough so you can see where the seabirds nest."

"Look at all that white stuff."

"That's years and years of buildup of bird droppings from the millions of birds. We won't go too close."

"I don't need a close-up. I'll take your word for it."

He grinned. "Smart girl." He slowly edged to the entrance to some of the caves before taking them around the island.

"There are birds everywhere." Laurette looked at the rolling green hills and scrub trees. "Like so much of Alaska, it's beautiful." She put her hand up, anticipating his comment. "I know, I won't say that in the dark of winter. Everyone keeps telling me that."

"I don't know. I think we have the dark days of winter so we appreciate all this beauty when we can see it."

"Kind of like Jesus. He's always there, but when life gets dark we don't always see Him." She gave him a thoughtful look.

He nodded. "Something to think about." He brought the boat close to the gap leading into open water. "Let's run out and take a look. If it's not too rough, we can try to find an early silver salmon or two."

"You mean into the ocean?"

"It's a calm day. Shouldn't be too bad, and we'll only go a

little way down the coast. I know a good fishing hole."

"You're the captain."

Ryan sped up and took them along the windward side of Kruzof Island. He slowed and took the boat into a large inlet. "More calm inside where it's protected, and I've caught some good-sized fish here."

"Let's give it a try." Laurette pulled the fishing poles from their storage place at the side of the boat.

Ryan laid out the proper lures. "I'll show you what to do to rig a pole to catch salmon." He took her fishing pole and pulled out line.

Laurette watched intently.

"The flasher moves in the water to attract the fish. Then he sees the green squid and smells the strip of fish."

"If you say so." She grinned and stood to let line out behind the boat.

"Let me put the motor in gear. Then you can put line out."

Laurette followed his directions, put the pole in the holder on the gunwale, and started to sit down.

"Can you take the wheel while I get my gear ready?"

She slid past him into the seat in front of the wheel. "Where do I go, Captain?"

"Try not to hit any rocks."

She stood quickly to look over the windshield. "Where are the rocks?" she asked in concern.

Ryan gave her a hug. "I'm teasing. Just head for where the inlet goes back into the ocean."

He got his line in the water and relaxed in the passenger seat. When they got close to the point, he told her to steer back to where they'd come from.

"Aren't you going to use the trolling motor?"

"We'll see how it goes. Currents are strong here, and we may need the power of the outboard."

The words were hardly out of his mouth when Laurette's

reel started to scream. "What do I do?" she yelled.

"Put the engine in neutral and grab that pole." As he spoke, Ryan started reeling in his line.

Laurette did as she was told. "Maybe I just got stuck on the bottom. It's not coming in." Her pole bounced. "I think I've got a whale," she squealed, working the pole up and down as Ryan had taught her.

"He's coming in," she said, reeling frantically as the fish swam toward the boat.

"Hold the line tight. You'll have to tire him out before we can get him into the boat."

She gave a sigh and pulled the tip of the pole up from the water again.

"Are you tired?"

She pursed her lips. "I'm not ready to give up yet."

It was nearly twenty minutes before Ryan could slip the net under the big fish and pull him into the boat.

Laurette sank onto the passenger seat. "My arms hurt."

"They should. That fish must weigh thirty pounds."

"Felt like three hundred."

Ryan got the hook out and the fish free of the net. "First one in the boat," he said, dropping the salmon in the fish box. He took Rette's hand and pulled her to her feet. "Good work." He pulled her into his arms and kissed her deeply.

"Let's catch another fish," she whispered, before he could kiss her again.

"That's what I like about my crew. Always willing to work," he quipped, letting go of her.

The mood of the day remained golden. Ryan caught a smaller salmon before the wind picked up and they headed to the lee side of the island in search of calmer water.

❧

"We forgot to eat lunch," Laurette said, searching under the bow for the small cooler.

"I didn't forget. Couldn't get you to quit fishing long enough to feed me," Ryan said with a mock growl. "This could cause a mutiny."

"It's the crew that mutinies, not the captain." She gave him a mischievous grin and pulled the cooler out of its hiding spot under her pack. "You want a ham sandwich, or are you too faint with hunger to take solid food?"

"Just give me the sandwich," he groused teasingly.

"Did you bring anything to drink? I could die of thirst in all this water."

"Now you're getting nasty just because you got the biggest fish." He spoke through a mouthful of sandwich. He motioned to another small cooler under the steering wheel. "Only the best for my lady."

She handed him a soda. "What? No chocolate milk?"

"When I fish, I drink soda."

She opened a can of cola and took a drink. "Seriously, I am thinking about that fish's future. Could I send some of it to my folks? My dad would love fish from Alaska."

"Especially if his little girl caught it." He took another sandwich.

"That would please him." Laurette opened the bag of chips she found.

"Why don't you send your folks the whole fish? They could have a party and show off your catch."

"Can I do that?"

"Since 9/11, individuals can't ship airfreight, but we could send it through SAM. We just sent one for a captain off one of the ships."

"I'd like my parents to see this beautiful country," she said, munching on a sandwich. "I don't think my dad has ever taken a vacation. All he does is work on the farm." She looked toward Mt. Edgecumbe. "This is so different from what my folks are used to. They see Mt. Spokane. Brian and

I used to ski there when we were kids, but we never thought about climbing it in summer."

"Do you miss your family?"

"I did when I first went to college. Now when I go home, it's not the same. We keep close by e-mail and phone calls, so I don't need to live close to them."

Maybe she *would* stay in Sitka. Ryan's hopes soared. He pushed his thoughts back and bunched up his sandwich bag. "I'd better get the fish cleaned while we're in still water." He fastened a tray over the side of the boat to hold the fish while he worked on them. "I'll cut the head off, but I'll leave your fish whole to ship. When we get back to the dock, I'll put it in my cooler and put crushed ice over it 'til we can pack and ship it tomorrow."

She gave him a dazzling smile. "That's a great plan. My dad will be pleased." She picked up the leftover food from lunch. The gulls circling the boat were only too happy to act as garbage disposals.

Ryan finished his job and cleaned the fish scales off the side and bottom of the boat. He turned to see Rette staring dreamily at the shoreline. Suddenly she jumped up. "Look. There's something moving on the beach."

"You're right." Ryan moved next to her and slipped his arm around her waist. "It's a black bear looking for something to eat."

She shivered and edged close to him. "As long as it isn't me."

He hugged her close to his side. "They don't bother people very often. It's the big grizzlies you have to look out for."

They stood, arms around each other, watching the animal lumber along the beach. When the bear moved into the trees, Rette looked up at Ryan. "I love this country. I don't ever want to leave."

"Me, either," he said pressing his lips to hers in a tender kiss.

sixteen

Ryan and Laurette packed her fish in a special box and shipped it airfreight to her parents. Laurette e-mailed her parents, advising them how to cook such a large piece of meat. "You can have a big barbecue and invite all your friends," she told her mother.

The next night, Laurette was cooking supper when the phone rang. She knew Ruth would answer, but when her friend called, "Come quick, Laurette, I think it's your mother," Laurette panicked.

Dropping the spoon she had in her hand, Laurette rushed to grab the phone. *Who's hurt? Why did Mother call?* "Hi, what's wrong?" she asked in one gasp.

Her father's chuckle quieted her fears. "We wanted you to know the monster fish has arrived. You really think that thing will fit on my barbecue?"

"Oh, Daddy, when Ruth said it was my mother, I thought something bad had happened."

"Not yet," her mother chimed in. "It may when your father attempts to cook fish for the neighborhood, though."

A warm glow filled Laurette to hear her parents' voices. She chilled quickly when her mother asked, "When are you coming home?"

"I don't know," she answered hesitantly. "I have a job 'til October."

"You really like it in Alaska, Rette?" her father asked.

"Yes, I do. I want you to come visit so you can see for yourselves."

"You mean take one of those cruises?"

"That or you can fly to Sitka and let me be your tour guide."

"We might just do that," her mother said. "Brian's doing more and more of the farmwork and planning. We could take a vacation."

"Not 'til the last of the winter wheat is in," her father fumed.

"I'll still be here," Laurette told him. *I'll be here if I still have a place to live, that is.*

"What about this boy you write about? Is he someone special?"

"He could be, Mom," she spoke quietly.

"Then we'd better make that trip to check him out," her father stated.

"Is he a good Christian?" her mother asked.

"We've been talking about our faith a lot, actually."

"That's wonderful, Laurette."

While that was true, she couldn't admit not knowing how far Ryan had come in that area. How could she explain that as a child he'd accepted Jesus as his Savior but had never genuinely embraced his Christianity?

Laurette forced her attention back to their call, again urged her parents to come see Alaska, and echoed their "I love you" as the call ended.

"Oh, Ruth, my parents may come to Sitka to see me!" She gave her friend a quick hug. "Now I should go see to supper before it's ruined."

When the two women sat down for their meal, Ruth asked, "Do you miss your home and family?"

"You're my family, here, and I feel like Sitka is home, too." She patted Ruth's wrinkled hand. Smiling, she continued, "I look forward to seeing my parents, but I don't have to have them close by to love them."

"I'm glad my John is here now that I need him." Ruth sighed.

"If my parents needed me, I would be there for them. Right now they have my brother to take over the farm. It's what we knew would happen sooner or later." She paused. "I don't know what I'm going to do."

Ruth squeezed Laurette's hand. "I know you will do the right thing."

I wonder if that includes Ryan, Rette pondered, clearing the table.

Sleep did not come easily. Laurette dreamed of her parents. What would they think of Ryan? Groggily she shut the alarm off and dragged herself to the shower.

By the time she entered the office, she felt ready for work. "What's new?" she asked Debbie.

"Tyler's gone, probably for the rest of the week. The head office sent him to settle some dispute over freight shipped to Seattle."

Laurette picked up the schedule. "Going to be busy. Where's Ryan?"

"He took customs papers aboard the ship that just set anchor. Can you take a look at this? I don't know what to do."

Laurette started her day trying to contact a pharmacy or doctor for a passenger who had dropped his bottle of heart pills overboard. "I had the nitro in my shirt pocket when I leaned over the rail," the man apologized.

"It's a good thing losing the pills didn't make him have a heart attack and need them," his wife fretted.

"I'm sure the medical team on board had more, and your husband would have been fine. Would you spell the name of the doctor for me, please?"

She and Ryan kept busy, so it was afternoon before they were both in the office at the same time. He was hanging up the phone when she walked in, and he looked frazzled.

"Problems?" she asked, filling a coffee mug.

"That was the cruise director of that special tour ship

due in Friday. He got word the entertainer who was due to join the ship in Sitka has canceled. He expects me to find a replacement overnight."

"You could change your career and play the piano aboard ships for a while," she quipped.

He scowled. "I don't know the first thing about finding an entertainer."

"You want me to go with you? You play and I'll sing. But I don't think we would make it through the first number before my singing had the audience walking out."

"You are not helping," he growled, the smirk on his face contradicting him.

"Can't you call a booking agency in Seattle and have them fly someone up here?"

Ryan sighed. "I thought of that, but this cruise director wants a native Alaskan."

"Why?"

He shook his head. "Who knows? I've never dealt with this cruise line before. It's small, and they do special study type programs. The captain wants to expose his passengers to native entertainment."

"Anything in particular?"

"He wants a native who will sing the songs of his people."

"I could call the Pioneer Home and see if anyone there could sing. Better yet, let's call the Sitka Community House. They have Tlingit storytellers and dancers."

"Go for it. I've got to get a pilot on board a ship since Mike's got his tug busy hauling freight."

"That gives me another idea. Ruth has talked about Mike's brother doing background music for television ads. Think she said his name was Paul. I'll call her and find out where he is."

Ryan looked dubious. "You think she'll be able to remember?"

"Won't know 'til I try."

"I've got to pick up the pilot at the dock. See you later."

Ryan grabbed his jacket and ran down the stairs.

Laurette dialed Ruth's number. "I need your help."

She could hear the pleasure in her friend's voice. "What could I possibly do for you?"

"Didn't you tell me Esther had a son who became a musician?"

"You mean Paul? He used to live in Seattle but moved back to Sitka when he retired."

"How old is he?" Laurette asked, wondering why the man was retired.

"Oh, he did real well in television, but he didn't like that life and came back here. Sometimes he fishes with John. He and my son are the same age."

Laurette explained the captain's request, then asked, "Do you think your nephew could help us?"

"Why don't you call Emmy? She would know how to contact Paul."

"Thank you, thank you, Ruth. You just may have solved a huge problem."

By the time Ryan got back a couple of hours later, Laurette had contacted Paul Littlefield. "He's willing to talk about this, but he says he is out of the entertainment business," she told Ryan with a chuckle. "Sounds like he didn't like playing backup to some of the prima donnas in show business."

"We'd better go meet him and see what kind of guy he is. Where is Paul now?"

"He's at Mike and Emmy's house."

"Hold the fort, Debbie, while we go hire a singer."

ða

Paul Littlefield turned out to be a personable man. Emmy had tapes of some of his work. "He even has songs he has written himself," she told Ryan.

Laurette thought Paul looked like his cousin John. His dark hair had a few strands of gray. He smiled easily, showing white teeth in a tanned face. He'd be good with an audience. She looked at Ryan, who nodded imperceptibly.

"There's one catch," Ryan told the man. "The cruise director wants you to wear a tux."

"No way." Paul's deep laugh rippled through the room. "Can you see me in a tux singing folk songs?"

"Not really," Ryan agreed.

"We'll just tell the cruise director that Paul will wear a native costume," Laurette said.

"And what's that?" Ryan asked.

She grinned. "Jeans, a plaid shirt, and red suspenders. This guy is good, and the audience won't care how he's dressed."

Paul shook Ryan's hand. "I like it. I'll do it." He turned to Laurette. "You're as smart as Aunt Ruth says. John sings your praises every time I fish with him. I agree with both of them." He took her hand in both of his. "Thanks for thinking of me. I'll do a good job for you."

≈

On the way back to the office, Laurette told Ryan about the call from her parents.

"You really think they'll come to Sitka?"

"I hope so," she said excitedly. "They've never taken a vacation before." She looked out the window toward the harbor. "I want them to see Sitka."

I'm not sure I want them to meet me, Ryan thought. It was late when he left the office that night. Driving home, he mulled over Laurette's news. What if her parents came to take her home? How likely was that? Her parents couldn't make their twenty-three-year-old daughter do anything. But he knew she loved them and would probably do what they asked.

Unless she loves me more. What if they didn't like him? What could he offer their daughter? A broken-down old trailer house?

Ryan sighed deeply and turned on the stereo as he headed for the kitchen. He opened a can of chili and dumped it in a pan. He picked up his Bible to read while his dinner heated.

He turned to the bookmark and read, paused, then reread Psalm 84:12. "O Lord of hosts, blessed is the man who trusts in You!"

That's the answer. I have to learn to put my trust in Jesus. Completely, no holding back.

Ryan continued to flip through the book of Psalms, reading bits and pieces until he smelled his supper burning.

He put the Bible down while he ate his scorched chili out of the pan. He smiled, remembering Laurette taking on the job of finding an entertainer for the cruise director. "We make a good pair," he muttered, putting the pan in the sink to soak. That man even bought the native costume idea. He shook his head and chuckled.

He plopped in his chair and picked up the Bible. *Trust and faith. I keep hearing those words. Will Jesus tell me if I should try fishing to make a living?* He sighed. *I just wish I had become a marine pilot. They make a good living, and there's always work for them.* He opened the Bible to Psalm 84 again. *I'll use the computer in the office to look up the requirements to be a pilot.* He looked around his trailer. "It's not too bad," he muttered. "If Rette would be willing to live here while I get my marine pilot's license, it might work out."

He read the psalm again. "I'm willing to try it, Lord. I will put my trust in You. Now I just have to learn how to hear Your answer."

seventeen

Ruth glowed in the praise Laurette heaped on her. "I'm so glad you sent us to Paul. He's perfect to entertain on the cruise ship."

"I'm sure he'll do a good job. He was Esther's most artistic child. She felt bad when he moved south, but she had her other children here." Ruth chuckled. "There are lots of Littlefields in Sitka."

Later, Laurette read to Ruth. They talked a little bit about the Scriptures before Ruth started to nod and her eyelids began to droop. Things had gone well for several weeks. Ruth loved the attention of the phone calls and having her nieces and nephews coming to visit. She seemed content to stay at home and not wander off.

After her friend went to bed, Laurette sat on the window seat enjoying the view. She realized the days were getting shorter as she watched the streaks of color from the approaching sunset.

And I still haven't decided what I'm going to do when my job ends.

What about Ryan? Again she thought about the difference in their faith. No, he definitely had faith. They'd prayed together. He'd even been the one to suggest prayer on several occasions.

Laurette had often prayed that the Lord would not let her fall in love with a non-practicing Christian, an unequally yoked relationship. And she knew she wouldn't consciously pursue someone who didn't follow Jesus. She trusted the Lord to show her if a relationship with Ryan would be unequally yoked, but she was still responsible for her own choices. *Lord Jesus, please show me what to do.*

With a sigh, she left her seat by the window and prepared for tomorrow. Work kept her busy, and she knew she would miss the excitement and challenge when it ended.

⋧

Ryan was already gone when she arrived early the next morning.

"Can you take this?" Debbie called, holding out the phone.

Laurette took it and listened to the caller's request. "Give me the address, and I'll be right there." She hung up the phone. "Are all the company vehicles out?" she asked Debbie.

"Tyler left the truck at the airport, and Ryan's got the van."

"I'm going to use my truck to pick up some freight."

She drove to the address the man had given her. She watched as they loaded crates into her little truck. *Hope there's room,* she thought. Her cell phone rang.

"Where are you?" Ryan asked.

"Picking up rabbit food."

"What?"

"We got a call from the barge operator. They had crates of lettuce for a ship, and their truck broke down."

"So what's this about rabbit food?" Ryan sounded really confused.

Laurette giggled. "They must have a lot of rabbits on that ship to go through this much lettuce. I'm not sure it will all fit in my truck."

"Your truck! You think it can handle all that weight?"

"I'll let you know in about forty-five minutes. They're through loading here, and I'm on my way to the dock where the ship's crew will pick it up."

"Call me as soon as you get there," Ryan insisted.

"Yes, Boss." Laurette disconnected.

An hour later, she walked into the office. "The rabbits will eat well tonight," she announced.

"Rette." Ryan turned as if to touch her but looked at

Debbie and must have changed his mind. "Did you have any problems?"

"No. My truck did just fine."

Ryan shook his head. "That's because there were no hills."

"Diane wants you to call," Debbie told Laurette, breaking up their conversation.

"When can you come for lunch?" Diane asked when Laurette phoned her.

"Looks like I could grab an hour off tomorrow. Will that work for you?"

❧

"Come see my mouse," David urged when Laurette arrived the next day.

"Mouse?" Laurette looked at Diane.

"He's cute and small—the kind of pet I like. He's supposed to stay in his cage, but you know kids."

"He likes to hide in my hair," Katie told her.

After inspecting the small white creature, the women sat down to enjoy a salad and tea. The children had sandwiches in front of the television.

"We need to plan a camping trip," Diane announced.

"Ryan and I have talked about hiking Mt. Edgecumbe."

"Good. There's a cabin on Kruzof Island. We could stay there, and the trail up the mountain is right behind the cabin."

"Could all of us go?"

Diane sighed. "It will take some planning to get Tyler away, but let's try. I'll get him to set the date, and then I'll contact the forest service to rent the cabin for a night. Do you have a sleeping bag?"

Laurette shook her head. "I don't have any camping gear."

"No problem. We have lots of extras. What will we take for food?"

"I could make a pot of stew if we have a way to heat it up," Laurette offered.

The time flew as the women planned menus. "I'll sit down with Tyler tonight and get him to name a date."

Laurette looked at the kitchen clock. "If I don't get back, I won't have a job." She quickly hugged the kids good-bye. "I'll come see your mouse again soon," she promised David.

"Her name is Francine," David reminded Laurette.

"See." Katie pushed back the hair on her neck, and a small pink nose peeked out.

Diane shook her head at Laurette. "I'll call you when I have a date."

"Thanks for lunch." Laurette waved as she left.

❧

"Tyler tells me we're going camping," Ryan said the next morning.

"Do we have a date?"

"You mean to climb Mt. Edgecumbe?"

Laurette felt her face burn. "I didn't mean to—that is, I meant do we have a date. For camping." She saw the mischief sparkle in his eyes and knew he was teasing her.

Ryan gave her a quick hug on his way to the coffeepot. "Tyler said Saturday after next. We'll go out that morning, spend the night at Fred's Creek, and hike the next day." He filled his cup. "Tyler, Diane, and the kids will pack up the camp and come back in the company boat. You and I will take my boat over and come back when we get back from climbing."

"Diane and I started planning menus. I don't have any camping gear, but she has a sleeping bag I can use."

"I'll give you a waterproof bag to pack your clothes in." He looked at her feet. "Those boots will be fine to hike in." He gave her a silly grin. "I'll even loan you a bear bell."

"Okay, what's the joke? I can see it in your eyes."

"If you use a bear bell and register the color, the authorities will know which bear ate you by the color of the bell in their scat."

"You're not funny." Then she thought for a moment. "Seriously, should I carry mace?"

"If you want to make a bear mad, that would be the way to do it. First you get close enough to spray him, and then you try to run faster than he does."

"I'll leave you in charge of bear protection. I'll stick to cooking supper for the group."

⁂

The Saturday of the trip dawned clear. The group met at the dock and packed the two boats. The company boat was bigger, so most of the gear went in it. Ryan and Laurette took only their own packs.

"I brought you a float coat," Diane said as she handed Laurette a red jacket.

"What's that for? I took warm clothes and rain gear."

"It's a float coat. If you go in the water, you pull this little tab. The gas cartridge fills the coat with air and keeps you floating."

"Thanks. I'll put it up front with the other life jackets."

Tyler and Diane loaded the kids into the boat and took off. They waved as Ryan started to back his boat down the ramp. "See you there," Tyler shouted.

Ryan and Laurette were soon out of the harbor. "You ordered up good weather again," Ryan said as they stood together, looking over the windshield.

Laurette looked at the boat speeding across Sitka Sound ahead of them. "They'll get there first."

"We'll be there right after them to help haul stuff to the cabin."

They seemed to head right to Mt. Edgecumbe, but as they neared the island, Laurette looked from the shore to Ryan. "How do you know where to land?"

"When we get a little closer, you'll see a stream coming in. Just to the left of it is a sandy beach we can pull onto. I'll moor the boat out after we get unloaded."

"Oh, I see the cabin." Laurette pointed to the weather-beaten A-frame set back against the tree line.

By the time Ryan edged his boat onto the beach, David and Katie were racing up and down shouting a welcome. Laurette had brought short rubber boots to wear in the boat. She jumped out to help pull the boat up on the sand.

It didn't take long for the adults to carry all the necessary gear to the cabin. Laurette looked at the rustic building.

"We'll keep the camp stove out here," Diane said, putting a metal case on a stump.

"Takes a lot of stuff for overnight," Laurette marveled, seeing the boxes and coolers on the cabin floor. "What can I do to help?" she asked Diane.

"Get Ryan to hand you the sleeping bags; we can spread them out later." She pointed to a ladder on the wall. "There are mats to go under them. Not exactly a feather bed, but better than sleeping on the hard floor."

It didn't take the women long to get the cabin settled. Diane told Laurette the men would moor the boats on lines that would let them float as the tide came in but not get loose.

"Daddy, Daddy, David says he saw a bear!" Katie came racing into the cabin.

"Daddy's down by the water. Where's your brother now?"

"He's gone to hunt the bear." Katie's voice quivered with fear.

Diane shook her head. "Your brother is such a tease!" She knelt and took Katie in her arms. "Katie, the bears won't hurt you. Just stay in the open. Play on the beach, and they won't come out of the woods."

The little girl sniffed.

"I'll come with you, Katie," Laurette offered. "Did you see any paw prints in the sand?"

The little girl shook her head.

"Did you find any pretty shells on the beach?"

"I didn't look," came the weak answer.

"Then let's go see what we can find."

As they started down the beach, the men came back toward the cabin. "Have you seen David? Katie's worried about him." Laurette said.

"He's over there with a shovel." Tyler pointed over his shoulder. "Why?"

"He told Katie he was going to hunt bears," Laurette explained.

"No bears today," her dad told her. "With all the noise you kids make, they're miles away by now." He patted his daughter's head.

Some of the little girl's enthusiasm returned. "We're going to find shells," she told her father.

"Looks like your brother is digging a hole."

"I'll go check on him," Ryan offered.

Tyler headed for the cabin while Laurette, Katie, and Ryan walked the beach toward David.

"What are you building?" Ryan asked David.

"A bear trap." He tossed another shovel full of sand on the pile he'd started. "When that bear walks down the beach, he's going to fall in my hole."

Ryan and Laurette continued to play with the children until Diane called to let them know lunch was ready.

Entering the cabin, Laurette saw sleeping bags on the two bunks against the walls of the main floor.

"You and I will give the upstairs to the men and kids. We'll sleep down here," Diane told her, putting a paper plate of sandwiches on the table. "I've got a basin of water on the shelf to wash your hands." She herded the children toward the wash water. Katie crawled into her mom's sleeping bag and fell asleep before she finished her sandwich. David ran out the door, sandwich in hand.

Walking the beach after cleaning up the lunch scraps, Laurette and Ryan found him sound asleep in his bear trap.

The couple stopped to look back at Sitka. The sun shone on the streaks of snow still visible on the mountain peaks. The lower hills were covered with Sitka spruce. Laurette could hear the low sound of wind in the trees towering behind them. "It's got to be a bit of paradise," she whispered.

"Tide's out." Ryan pointed to rocks on the shore she hadn't seen when they landed. "Let's walk out on them."

They found a spot at the top of a slab of rock and sat to drink in the beauty around them. Ryan took her hand. No words were necessary. They could communicate by touch. *I belong here,* Laurette said silently. She looked at Ryan. *I belong with him.*

As if reading her thoughts, he pulled her into his embrace. Their lips touched in sweet communion.

Katie's laughter broke the spell. "Look, Mommy. The bear caught David."

That was a short nap, Laurette thought, slightly embarrassed.

Diane and Tyler followed their daughter to where David stretched with a sleepy yawn.

"Up and at 'em, you two. If you want a fire tonight, we have to find driftwood."

Beachcombing and ball games filled the afternoon. By evening, Laurette's stew warmed on the camp stove while Ryan and Tyler worked to get a fire going. They sat on the logs they'd placed around the fire pit and ate their supper.

"The only way to clean the dishes," Ryan declared, tossing his paper plate into the flames.

Laurette watched Ryan take some bread from the kids' plates and crumble it on a path from the creek to the cabin. "Are you baiting bears?" she asked him quietly while the children were busy toasting marshmallows.

"It's bait but not for bears."

Laurette remembered a story her mother had told her and repeated it for the children. They sat quietly listening. Ryan put his finger over his lips and pointed to the path from the creek. "It's my martin."

A small brown animal about the size of a large cat crept out of the brush and sniffed the bread crumbs. It stopped and looked toward the fire, its eyes gleaming in the light. Soon it moved until it could reach more crumbs. The martin ate all the bread and then looked with its nose in the air as if to say thank you before scurrying back into the brush.

"*Your* martin?" Tyler asked.

Ryan nodded. "I wasn't sure he'd still be here. It's been years since I've been out here at night. Maybe not the same one I remember, but must be his family's in charge of keeping the campground clean."

They all chuckled, and Diane rose to get the sleepy children inside and ready for bed.

"I have to get back early tomorrow. Diane and I will pack up after breakfast and see you two back in town," Tyler said, getting up to follow his wife.

"We'll be up early to start to the top." He took Laurette's hand. "Have your clothes laid out. I'll wake you when I get up."

"I've got snacks in my day pack. Diane had water bottles for us."

Ryan bent over to kiss her forehead. "I'll see you at dawn."

eighteen

Laurette opened her eyes when she felt Ryan's lips on her forehead. "Mmmm, nice alarm clock." She stretched her arms over her head.

"Up and at 'em, lazybones. I'll go get the coffee started." With a final kiss he went outside.

Laurette had clothes laid out and dressed quickly. When she saw the long johns, she decided they would be too warm hiking, so she stuffed them in her pack.

"Just leave the sleeping bag. We'll roll it later," came sleepy instructions. With a yawn Diane added, "Have a nice day, and call me when you get back to town."

"Feel like I'm leaving you with all the work."

"Not a problem. Been nice to get away from the house. Kids sure have had fun." Laurette watched Diane pull the sleeping bag back over her shoulders as she reminded Laurette, "Don't forget the water bottles in the cooler."

Ryan had coffee perking on the camp stove. "I think it's ready," he told Laurette when she joined him.

"I brought muffins and fruit from the cabin. Are there cups out here?"

"Yup." Ryan poured them coffee. They munched their breakfast while gazing across the water to Sitka.

"Ready?" he asked, setting his cup on the log.

She nodded. "I've got my day pack with snacks and a sweatshirt if I need it."

"Let's go."

Laurette followed Ryan on the path behind the cabin. She could hear the gurgling stream off to their right. The trail ascended at an easy incline. The trees were dense, so Laurette couldn't see much, even when she looked up to the tops. Squirrels chattered at them. Putting one foot in front of the other, she trudged behind Ryan. His lanky form seemed to meld with the brush. *He's at home here. It's so peaceful it's easy to forget I only have a temporary job. I could just keep following this man forever.*

"You want to take a break?"

Laurette flexed her shoulders. "I'd love a drink of water." She slipped the pack off her back.

"Let me carry that for a while." Ryan took the pack, removed a bottle of water, and offered her a drink.

She noticed Ryan checking the sky and thought maybe he saw something in the trees. "You spot an eagle up there?"

"No, just trying to keep an eye on the weather."

"How? All I see is an occasional sunbeam through the branches."

"I'm watching the treetops to see if the wind is blowing."

They continued walking. "There'll be more open spots, and you may find some soggy places," he cautioned.

So far, all Laurette had seen was soft dust. Her boots were covered with it. Fifteen minutes later Ryan stopped and pointed to the trail ahead. "We may detour here and not wade through that." He pointed to a marshy area.

As they continued he went close to the marsh and stooped down. "Come see this."

Laurette squatted down next to him. "What is it?"

He pointed.

"Oh, that's huge. What kind of animal has feet that big?"

"Grizzlies."

"You're serious? There are bears that big on this trail?" A knot of fear twisted her stomach.

He grinned and gave her a quick kiss. "I'll protect you."

"How?" She held her hand over the bear print. "It's twice

as big as my hand."

"Had a friend shoot one on Kodiak Island that had claws five inches long."

"Ryan, you're scaring me."

He pulled her into his arms. "You're okay. That print is old and the bear is long gone."

She sighed. "I trust you. Lead on."

He gave her a hug before starting back up the trail.

Laurette did trust Ryan. She felt safe being near him. His touch left her tingling.

They hiked for another hour. This time Ryan stopped in a clearing. They could catch a glimpse of the water below. *It doesn't sparkle*, Laurette thought. She looked up and saw there were clouds moving in to cover the sun. *Hope we don't get wet.*

"A little farther up there's a lean-to. We can stop there to have lunch."

Laurette noticed him check the sky again. *He'll know what to do.* She resisted the niggling doubts trying to sneak into her mind.

"It feels good to sit down," she said when they reached the lean-to.

"Some people spend the night in this shelter." Her eyes followed his gaze as he looked at the broken shakes on the roof. "Could get wet if it rained. I think we'll just have lunch and move on," he joked. "I like the cabin at Fred's Creek better. Kind of rustic but fun."

She smiled. "Great place for the children."

"There are more forest service cabins. Some people use them for hunting and others for fishing. I came out to Fred's Creek with my folks when I was little."

"You don't have family here anymore," she said sadly. He smiled. "I'm used to it." He reached to take her hand. "But it's nice to have a friend to share with."

They munched on trail mix and dried fruit. "There's another bottle of water," she told him.

"Save it for the trip down." He stood to look around. "That wind is getting stronger. I think we'd better forget going to the top and start back. Could be a rough crossing to Sitka."

Hearing the urgency in his voice, Laurette quickly gathered up their belongings and prepared to follow his lead. "We'll make the top another day," she announced cheerfully as they set off down the trail.

He set a fast pace. Laurette could feel the pull in the back of her legs and knew she would be stiff in the morning.

"Need a break?" he asked.

She caught her breath and opened the last bottle of water. She wiped the back of her hand over her mouth and handed the bottle to him. "Are we going to be all right?"

He looked up. The trees were dense, but they could see the tops swaying in the wind. "We'll take it slow, but it may be a rough ride."

Before they broke into the clearing by the cabin, they could hear the surf pounding the beach. Laurette caught her breath when she first saw the high waves cresting in whitecaps. Fear clutched her heart. Instinctively she reached to touch Ryan's arm. "I can't see the boat."

"It's pulling on the ropes, but it's holding where I moored it." He pointed to the white boat bobbing in the gray and white water. He put his arm around her waist. "Get dressed in warm clothes and your rubber boots. Bring your pack and meet me on the beach." With a quick squeeze he headed for the boat.

Laurette ran to the cabin. Diane had left it clean. Rette's pack lay on her bunk. She pulled a sweatshirt over the cotton turtleneck sweater she wore and zipped her vest on top of that. She switched the leather hiking boots for the short rubber boots. She quickly pulled on her rain pants and stuffed the rest of her belongings in the waterproof pack, then rolled it down and fastened it tight. She shut the cabin door behind her and tried to run in the loose sand in spite of wearing rubber boots.

Ryan stood in the boat wearing his mustang suit. The orange survival suit sent a new charge of fear circulating through her spine. He motioned for her to come over the bow. "I can't get any closer to shore," he yelled above the roar of the surf.

Laurette never paused. She plunged into the water and reached to grab the rail on the bow. She felt the icy water fill her boots as she tossed her pack on the deck and struggled to pull herself up after it. With a final effort she got her feet over the side and crawled through the opening in the windshield.

Ryan had grabbed the pack and tossed it under the passenger seat. He helped Laurette into the cabin before he closed the windshield and zipped the canvas to seal the top. He took her arm and shouted above the wind. "Can you find the float coat?"

She nodded.

"Get it on. I'm going to try to back us out without hitting any rocks."

Laurette dragged the jacket from its storage spot and zipped it on. It didn't have a hood like her raincoat, but she found a seaman's cap in the pocket. *It will have to do*, she thought as she pulled it over her hair. At least the bulky jacket kept the wind out.

She sat down as Ryan pulled the last rope free of the mooring buoy and put the motor in reverse. She didn't think she took a breath until she saw him turn toward open water. *We made it through the rocks. Thank You, Lord.*

Ryan sat with one hand on the wheel and the other hand working the manual windshield wiper.

Laurette peered into the gloom and could see nothing

but water sheeting off the glass in front of her. The farther they got from land, the rougher the water became. The boat would climb up a wave only to fall into the trough on the other side. Each time the bottom dropped with a crash, Laurette felt the shudder. *Surely the boat will break up.* She fought back panic.

Ryan appeared to concentrate on where they were going. He did glance at her once with a reassuring smile. The constant wail of the wind made conversation impossible.

Laurette closed her eyes. Her mind would not work beyond the repeated prayer, *God, have mercy.*

Waves washed over the top of the boat, sending water through every opening it could find. More than once Laurette felt the cold water run down her neck. She didn't know if it was the cold or fear that made her shiver. She was glad Ryan had his mustang suit. He would stay warm and dry and get them safely into the harbor.

The wind whipped across the top of the waves, sending spray to lash against them. Laurette felt like she was in a washing machine set on high. She held on to the bar fastened to the dashboard. Nothing was left on the shelf itself. Everything had been knocked to the deck.

Ryan leaned over where he could shout in her ear. "I'm going to head for Beally Rocks. We'll get some protection from the wind there." He patted her cheek with his wet hand.

She tried to smile encouragement but knew it was a weak effort. She tried to pray, but words would not form. She continued to repeat her silent plea for the Lord's mercy. *He stilled the winds for the disciples,* she reasoned. *He can save us now.*

She looked back when the angle of the boat caused the propeller to come out of the water. It screamed in protest. Laurette screamed when she saw the water level in the back of the boat. Tugging Ryan's arm, she pointed. She knew they were going to sink.

Ryan put his mouth next to her ear. "The bilge pump can't keep up. I need you to keep the boat pointed into the waves. If you don't, we could capsize. I have to bail some water out."

With grim determination, Laurette slid into the seat behind the wheel. It took every ounce of her strength to hold the boat steady. The waves grabbed at the boat and tried to wrench it out of her control. She pumped the windshield wiper, but it did little to help her view. She could hear Ryan scrape the bucket against the floor again and again. The rushing waves blotted out any sound of him emptying water over the side. She could only hope he could keep them from sinking.

Laurette strained to see ahead. How close were they to the rocks? "I don't want to run into them," she muttered.

Her arms ached. The tension in the rest of her body blotted out the cold that made her teeth chatter. She felt Ryan's hands on her back. His touch gave her courage. She looked up at him.

He motioned her to move back to the passenger seat. "I'll take over."

She could read his lips and slid back to her seat. She watched him check the compass and thought with a start, *I never looked to see if I kept us on the same course.*

She watched him strain to see ahead.

"Must be getting close," he yelled. "I think I can make out the shadows."

The motor coughed. At first Laurette thought the prop had come out of the water again. No. It happened again. It was a cough and a sputter.

Ryan looked worried. He tried to change the speed. This time the motor sounded like it would stop completely. The next time it did.

She watched with her heart in her throat while Ryan tried

again and again to restart it. She caught the glimpse of a shape go by the side of the boat. Trying to see in the wind-whipped rain, she forgot the motor until the silence broke her concentration.

"We made Beally Rocks. Should find some relief from the wind here."

Without the motor running, Laurette could hear him clearly. She pointed at the still mechanism and asked, "What's wrong with it?"

"Could be water in the carburetor or fuel line. Could be electrical. I don't know."

"Will we crash in the rocks?" she asked, voicing the fear that clutched her.

He shook his head and went to the stern to lower the trolling motor. "I think I can control us with this."

"Will it get us home?"

He shook his head and grimaced. "Better get the VHF radio out. We need help."

nineteen

Laurette dug through the things stored under the bow until she pulled out an orange waterproof pack.

"Get the radio out and hand it to me. I'll call the Coast Guard," Ryan told her.

He leaned against the corner of the stern while he tried to control their course with the trolling motor.

She watched as he pulled out the antenna and dialed up the correct frequency. "This is Ryan Nichols. We are drifting inside Beally Rocks. Our outboard motor has gone out, and I am trying to keep us off the rocks with a trolling motor. We need assistance."

"Message has been received, Mr. Nichols. We have an emergency. . .tourist boat. . .Lazeria Island. Will respond. . .soon. . .possible." A crackle of static ended the transmission.

"What does that mean?" Laurette asked, trying to keep the terror out of her voice.

She saw a fleeting glimpse of fear in Ryan's eyes before he gave her a brief smile.

"They'll get to us when they can."

She gulped down the panic trying to rise in her throat. "Are we going to be all right?"

He nodded as he shoved the motor far to the right to try to avoid the surf crashing against a nearby rock.

The wind swept the rain over them sideways. Ryan hunched over as if to protect his face. Laurette stayed under what protection the canvas top offered the front seats.

Her feet were numb. She kept her cold hands in the pockets of the float coat. More than once she fingered the tab to pull the cartridge that would blow up the jacket so she would float in the water. Watching the looming rocks and hearing the waves crash against the shore mesmerized her. In her trance she continued to ask for God's mercy and protection.

&

Ryan watched Laurette. He knew she was cold and feared hypothermia had started. He felt helpless. *Dear God, have You given her to me only to take her away? Please keep her safe. I know if she goes in the water, she will die. Show me how to take care of her.* He saw the island looming in their path and tried to steer the heavy boat with the small engine. He kept the radio in a zippered pocket of his mustang suit. He'd turned the volume on high so he would hear it above the whine of the wind and lashing rain.

An hour passed. Laurette sat staring out the side of the boat. His efforts to call to her were snatched by the wind. He didn't dare leave the motor for a second. The looming rocks threatened them on all sides. At least the waves were not as high. They didn't continually climb and crash back down. Ryan's back ached where he tried to brace against the corner of the boat to remain on his feet. The constant movement of the currents made the unsteady deck treacherous.

The radio crackled. He grabbed it out of his pocket. "Ryan Nichols here."

"It's Mike, Ryan. Heard your call. Just coming out of Jamestown Bay. I'm on my way. Slow going, but hang on, kids; we'll be there in less than two hours."

Ryan looked at Laurette. He didn't know if it was rain or tears on her cheeks. Probably a mix. "Could you hear?"

She shook her head.

"Mike's on his way," he shouted.

She waved at the water, rocks, and surf around them. "Can we hold out until he gets here?" she yelled into the wind.

"All things are possible with God. We'll let Him navigate for us." He thought he saw a slight smile curve her lips. "Rette, try to move around a little. You need to keep your circulation going. Stomp your feet."

"I can't feel them." She tried to stand but grabbed the seat when the boat rocked to one side. She fell into the seat by the wheel. "Are you warm?" she shouted at him.

He patted his mustang suit. "That's what this thing is for. We need to get you one."

She nodded and laid her head back against the seat.

Ryan alternately watched her and where the boat was drifting. Was she asleep? How advanced was the hypothermia? He longed to hold her, but she was better off under the shelter provided by the canvas top than at the stern with him. *Please, Lord, take care of her.*

It seemed like an eternity before the shape of the tugboat appeared in the clouds that met the sea.

With great effort Ryan maneuvered his boat toward the tug. He had to move into open water where Mike could get close enough to throw them a line. Mike had brought the tug in on the lee side so the wind did not whip quite as hard.

"Just sit where you are," Ryan instructed Laurette, who had perked up at the sight of their rescuer.

Mike worked from the deck of the tug and Ryan from his until the ropes were securely holding the small fishing boat.

When the last rope had been secured, Mike called, "Is Laurette all right?"

"Yes," Ryan replied. He turned to help Laurette stand at the rail. She shivered in his arms. "She'll need help getting aboard."

Mike stepped back and returned with a large rope ladder. "Can you guide her up with this?"

Ryan stood behind Rette. "Just reach up and take the ladder. I'll be right behind you, holding you steady."

He felt her take a deep breath; then she reached out to grab the rope. Step by step they made it up the ladder to the deck. Mike scooped her into his arms and carried her inside the cabin. He sat her down on a bench. "Get her boots off and rub her feet. I'll get us headed for Starrigavan," Mike instructed.

Ryan knelt and pulled off Rette's soggy boots and socks. He grabbed a towel and started to rub blue feet.

"Oh, they burn," Laurette cried as the circulation started to come back.

Ryan spotted a coffeepot on top of the stove. "I'll heat us some coffee."

"I'll do it. You go help Mike. I'll be okay."

He smiled, kissed her forehead, and headed out the door.

"She'll be all right as soon as she gets warm," Mike told him when Ryan joined him.

Ryan shook his head. "If the boat had broken up and she'd gone in the water, she wouldn't have survived."

Mike clapped him on the back. "But it didn't. You did a fine job of keeping her safe."

"I didn't do it alone." He blinked back the tears that threatened to overflow.

"You had a lot of people praying for you."

Ryan straightened his back and went to where he could see over the side. His boat rode safely next to the tug.

"We'll go into the launch at Starrigavan," Mike told him again. "I radioed Tyler that we're on our way. He'll be there with the truck and your boat trailer."

"What happened to the Coast Guard? I called them hours ago."

"One of those sightseeing boats hit the rocks on St. Lazeria. The Coast Guard had all personnel out there saving the tourists. Last report on the VHF said only one got hurt. The rest are on their way back to Sitka." He grinned at Ryan.

"As soon as I heard your call, I let them know I would bring you in with the tug. Didn't want them to leave your boat to break up on the rocks."

"Thanks. I didn't think about the boat. I just wanted to get Rette safely back to land."

"Everything's under control. Why don't you go back and sit with her? Did you heat up the coffee?"

"She sent me up here. I'm sure she did, though. You want me to bring you a cup?"

Mike pointed to the thermos cup next to the wheel he used to control the tug. "Got plenty, thanks."

Laurette sat where he had left her. She had unzipped the jacket and pulled off the cap. He thought her face had more color. "Can you feel your feet?"

"Yes, and I can move my fingers and toes." She smiled. "No frostbite."

He saw the damp streaks on her sweatshirt. "But you're wet."

"I could use a hot shower right now."

He sat down beside her. "Tyler will be waiting with the truck and trailer. Would you be willing to stay at my place while we take the boat into the shop? The motors need to be flushed with fresh water as soon as possible to get the salt water out of the system. You could take a shower there. I'll pick up my car and be back to take you home."

"Where are we going?" She looked confused.

Ryan explained they were not going into Crescent Harbor. "We're going into the campground north of Sitka. That's why Tyler will be there. He's moved the boat trailer from where we left it. We go right by the mobile home park where I live on our way into town." He put his arm around her shoulders. "That way you get out of those wet clothes and into a hot shower quicker."

"Sounds good." She put her head on his shoulder. "I'm so tired."

"You worked hard to pray us to safety," he whispered, pulling her closer.

She sat up. "I didn't have enough faith. I was scared."

He looked into her beautiful, gold-flecked brown eyes. "Fear tests our faith. When Jesus told Peter to come out of the boat and walk on the water to Him, he did, but Peter's fear made him doubt, so he began to sink. Then he asked Jesus to save him, so Peter did have faith, but it was still weak."

"You've been reading the Gospel of Matthew."

"It took something very dramatic to convince the disciples Jesus was the Son of God. That story seems real personal to me now," he said and chuckled. "Rette, you didn't stop believing or praying, in spite of your fear. And I think I prayed harder because of my fear. God heard your pleas and mine, and we're headed back to safety."

Ryan pulled her close. "I could have lost you."

They looked up as Mike shouted, "We're coming in."

Ryan rushed to the wheelhouse.

"I'll take you in as close as I can. Will you be able to get your trolling motor going again? You'll need it to get the boat onto the trailer."

Ryan turned to Laurette, who had followed him. "Better keep praying. We aren't on land yet." He looked at her bare feet. "Can you pull those boots back on? We have to go down the ladder to my boat."

"Look for some dry socks in the cupboard over the bench," Mike told her.

Ryan climbed back into his boat. He looked up from untying ropes when he heard Laurette come to the rail of the tug. "Can you come down? I'll come partway up to meet you."

He watched her climb over the deck rail and put her feet on the rope ladder. He held her a moment longer than necessary after he helped her off the last rung and onto the boat. "You could have stayed on the tug. I could have picked you up in Jamestown Harbor."

"I want to stay with you." She clung to him until he had to go back to getting the boat loose.

Free of the tug, he waved to Mike and lowered the trolling motor into the water. It took several pulls on the starter rope, but it roared to life. Ryan guided the boat next to the dock at the launch site.

"Welcome home," Tyler called. He had the trailer backed down the ramp and ready to go. "Let me give you a hand, Laurette."

Ryan held the boat against the dock while she climbed out. "Go wait in the truck where you'll be warm," he told Rette.

The men maneuvered the boat onto the trailer. After Tyler had pulled it back up the ramp, Ryan took out the plug in back and watched as water gushed out.

"Took on some water, did ya?" Tyler quipped when he came back to help Ryan secure the boat to the trailer.

Moments later, Ryan slid into the cab next to Laurette and pulled her close to him. "Are you warm now?"

She put her head on his chest and murmured, "Yes."

◆

When they stopped in front of a small mobile home, Laurette sat up.

"The door isn't locked. The shower is down the hall on the right. You go on in. I'll get your pack out of the boat so you have dry clothes." He smiled. "Assuming you rolled and fastened the pack correctly." He walked her to the door and gave her a quick kiss on the forehead.

He returned with her pack, then said, "I'll be back soon."

Laurette pulled off her boots and hung the float coat in the porch entryway. Slowly she opened the door. She looked at the small but neat living room with a bookcase dividing it from the kitchen. Against one wall stood a small electric organ. She padded down the hall to the bathroom and started peeling off wet clothes. The shower felt wonderful. She let the hot water cascade down her back and warm her all the way through.

When she pulled a towel off the rack, she spotted a terrycloth robe on the back of the door. She put it on. The sleeves hung over her hands, and the hem almost dragged on the floor. She drank in Ryan's scent as she wrapped the robe almost twice around her body before tying it. With a towel around her wet hair, she went back to the living room where she had left her pack.

The davenport looked so inviting that she sank down onto it. The pillow at the end felt perfect as she curled up and fell into a deep sleep.

twenty

Ryan pulled off his boots and hung his mustang suit on the peg next to Rette's float coat. He opened the door and reached to turn on the stereo. His hand stopped and so did his heart when he saw Rette. She lay curled up on his davenport sound asleep. He tiptoed close to her. The towel around her head had come off, leaving her damp hair loose to fall into ringlets. Her bare feet peeked out of his terrycloth robe. He moved quietly to the spare bedroom and brought back a blanket to spread over the sleeping girl. He watched her breathe and thanked God she had survived.

Finally, he backed away from her and walked softly down the hall. When he went into the bathroom, he stumbled over her stack of wet clothes. He put them in a plastic bag before taking a shower.

He stood in the hot water trying to wash away some of the exhaustion. It had been a long day.

Dressed in jeans and a flannel shirt, Ryan went back to check on Laurette. She stirred in her sleep. The nervous flutter in his stomach was not from hunger.

When Rette opened her eyes, he dropped to his knees beside the davenport. Overwhelming emotion took his voice away. He gently kissed her lips. "How do you feel?" he whispered.

She stretched and sat up, swinging her feet to the floor beside him. "I'm finally warm. How long did I sleep?"

He glanced at his watch. "Little over an hour."

"I should let Ruth know where I am."

"The radio has been busy. Everyone who listened during

the storm knows we are back safe in Sitka. Mike and John have kept in contact, and I think John is with Ruth now. When you feel up to it, we'll go see her."

Laurette looked up at him. He thought he could drown in her light brown eyes. He took her hands. "Rette, I could have lost you. I've never prayed so hard in my life." His voice shook. "I love you. I don't ever want to lose you."

He watched a tear run down her cheek.

He pulled her to her feet. *She's so small and yet so strong*, he thought. He kissed the tear away. "I have nothing to offer you. I don't even have a steady job, but I want to marry you."

Laurette put her arms around his neck and laid her head against his chest. "I love you, too."

He ran his hands through her unruly hair. "Does that mean you'll marry me?"

She smiled and nodded before his lips came down on hers. An eternity later Ryan stepped back, placing his hands on her shoulders. "Do you think you could live in this place until I can find a better job?"

"I don't care where I live as long as I'm with you."

Laurette wiggled her bare feet and looked at the bulky robe tied around her. She giggled. "This is not the romantic setting I dreamed of when I promised to marry the man I love."

"As long as I'm in that picture, I don't care how you look." He took her fluttering hands.

"I'd still like to get dressed."

He picked up her pack on the floor. "I hope you have dry clothes. I don't think anything of mine would fit any better than that robe."

&

Laurette opened the pack in the bathroom. She pulled out yesterday's jeans and sweatshirt and tried to shake the sand into the wastebasket instead of on the floor. *Married. I'm going to get married.* The thrill that zinged through her blotted out the fact she was putting on dirty clothes to greet her beloved. *If he loves me like this, he will always love me,* she thought, brushing out her hair.

She carried her hiking boots back to the living room, but she had pulled socks over her bare feet. Ryan stood at the stove in the kitchen. Soft music played on the stereo. "You cook, too?" she asked.

"Soup out of a can. Are you hungry?"

"Yes. I guess it isn't true that you can live on love alone."

"If I don't find a better job, we may have to try."

She put her face against his flannel-clad back. "I've got my summer wages saved."

He turned to pull her into his embrace. "God will take care of us."

He sat in his big chair and she curled up on the davenport with their bowls of soup.

"I'll look for a job, too," she told him. "I don't think a biology degree is going to help much, but I can wait on tables."

"You have a job until October, and mine will last until November."

"How about a Christmas wedding?"

"We'll have lots of time for a honeymoon," he quipped.

"You can play for tips to keep us in food," she said as she laughed. "We'll find a way." She took his bowl and headed for the kitchen sink.

"Leave the dishes. I should get you home before John and Mike come looking for you."

The storm had moved on, but the rain still fell. Laurette moved as close as she could to Ryan in the little Volkswagen. Her heart sang with joy. *Thank You, thank You, Lord,* she prayed silently. *You've sent me a perfect husband.*

❧

When they entered the house, Ruth called out, "Is that you, Laurette? We've been waiting for you."

"Sorry, I fell asleep and didn't come right home."

Ruth looked puzzled. *Maybe she forgot I went camping,* Rette thought.

"I'm going to go live with Esther." Her friend's face was wreathed in smiles.

Laurette looked at John and saw his pained expression. "You're going to live where Esther used to live, Mother," he corrected. He motioned Ryan and Rette to a seat on the davenport. "I need to explain," he said. "I put Mother's name on the list to get a room at the Pioneer Home after her visit to the Pioneer Bar."

"When did I ever go to a bar?" Ruth protested.

"Just joking, Mother," he continued. "A room has become available, and Mother has decided it's time she went there." He took his mother's hand and sat on the arm of her chair. "She knew Aunt Esther was happy living at the Pioneer Home. And she knows many people who live there now."

Laurette looked at Ryan, who took her hand. "That's a good idea, John. How soon will you want me to move?"

"Oh, I want you to stay here," Ruth interjected. "Won't you live here and take care of my house?"

Confused, Laurette looked from John to Ruth.

"What Mother means is she wants to be able to come home." He put his hand up. "Not to stay but to visit. This has been her home for fifty years, and," he added, smiling, "this is the only way she's willing to leave it."

Laurette gulped and looked at Ryan. "I don't have a job after October."

John nodded. "I know. We'll just have to work things out. The important thing now is to get Mother moved and settled in her new home."

"Maybe we can rent it from you, John. I'm looking for a better job." He looked at Rette and saw her nod. "We're planning to be married."

"Congratulations!" John jumped up to shake Ryan's hand and give Laurette a hug. "Did you hear, Mother? Laurette and Ryan are going to get married."

Ruth beamed. "Oh, a wedding to plan. How exciting. I hope I can come."

"There won't be a wedding without you," Laurette said, kneeling by her friend's chair and taking her hands. "I have to have my special grandmother at my wedding." She stood, and Ryan put his arm around her waist.

"And I love talking with you about the Bible," he told Ruth.

"Do you read the Psalms like I told you?"

He smiled. "Yes, ma'am, I do."

The couple chatted with Ruth until she announced she felt tired. After she had gone to her room, John asked Ryan about the trip across from Fred's Creek.

While they talked, Laurette put her wet clothes in the washing machine. John rose when she came back. "Time I got home."

"How soon will Ruth move?" Laurette asked.

"She'll want to decide what she needs in her new home. There isn't any rush, but I'd like to get her settled by the first of the month."

"I'll help."

Ryan put his hand on her shoulder. "John and I have talked terms. He'll make it easy for us to buy Ruth's house."

She smiled and looked around the living room. "There's room for a piano."

"All we need is work."

"You can fish with me any time you want," John offered.

"Thanks. I'm sure the Lord will show us what He has in store for us," Ryan replied.

After John left, Ryan stifled a yawn. "You didn't get a nap," Laurette said, snuggling close to him on the davenport.

"It's been a long day. Did you realize it's after ten? We've been up since five."

"And it's been an amazing day." She put her head on his shoulder. "You saved my life."

"Is that why you're willing to marry me?" he teased.

"That and because I love you." She sat up straight. "I want to talk about so much with you, but I think we should both get some sleep."

"Why don't you sleep in tomorrow? Come to work late. Besides, Ruth will be excited to start packing to move."

"I want to call my mother."

"I wonder what my mother will say when I tell her I'm getting married," Ryan said.

"To someone she has never met." Then she added, "My parents haven't met you, either. This could be interesting."

"We've got a few wrinkles to iron out, but we'll do it together." He pulled her close and kissed her good night.

❧

"Mom?"

"Hello, dear. Good to hear your voice," Laurette's mother said. "Dad's out in the field."

"I wanted to talk to you."

"Is there a problem? Why are you calling in the morning?"

"No problems. I wanted to tell you first." She gulped and blurted out, "I'm getting married."

"When? This is so quick. Is it the boy you've written about?" The concern in her mother's voice sent a shiver through Laurette.

"Yes, it's Ryan. And I've known him since the first day I got to Sitka. I know you'll like him."

"If he makes you happy, your dad and I will welcome him to the family. Now tell me all about it. When did you decide, and what plans have you made?"

"He just asked me yesterday, so we don't have many plans

yet. But"—she hesitated—"I would like to be married in Sitka."

"Well, if it's what you want, we can work it out. Do you have a date?"

"No. I don't even have a job after October." She decided not to tell her mother Ryan's job ended in November. "I did think a Christmas wedding would be fun."

Her mother laughed. "At least we know your father won't be busy in the fields then."

"I wanted to talk to you alone, but I'll call tonight and tell Daddy."

"Do you want me to keep it a secret until then?"

"No, I want you to soften Daddy up so he doesn't demand I come home tomorrow." Laurette laughed.

"Now you know your father would never do anything like that. We trust you to pick out a good man to take care of you." Laurette heard the sigh. "Dad may not think he's good enough for you, but dads are that way about their little girls."

"Oh, Mom, I am so happy. I wish you were here."

"I'd like to be there to give you a big hug. Now you sit down and write me all that's going on. We can plan this wedding by e-mail. My little girl has grown up." Laurette heard the catch in her mother's voice.

"I love you, Mom. I've thought a lot about living so far away, but we'll visit often."

Her mom sighed across the phone lines. "Yes, we will."

"Keep Daddy in the house. I'll call back at eight your time tonight."

"We'll wait for your call. Love you."

Laurette went to work at noon.

Ryan came in soon after she reported for work. He kissed her forehead. "Did you get rested?"

"Yes, and I called my mother."

"Is the wedding off?"

She smiled up at him. "No, but we still have to tell my father."

"We? Does this mean you want me with you?"

"Would you, please?"

"It's proper that I ask for your hand in marriage. When do we do this?" Ryan asked.

"Tonight. I'll even cook supper for you."

He took her hand, sending tingles up her arm.

"Am I going to get any work out of the lovebirds anymore?" Tyler quipped.

Laurette felt her face grow hot. "You told everyone?" she accused Ryan.

"Just Tyler."

"And I came to work late." She apologized to Tyler.

"Congratulations on the engagement. As for coming in late, after yesterday I'm thankful you came in at all. Do you have any bad effects?" her boss asked.

She grinned. "The backs of my legs are stiff from the run back down Mt. Edgecumbe."

"Now that she's here, may I take her to lunch?" Ryan asked.

Tyler shrugged. "As long as she calls my wife as soon as she gets back. Diane wants to know for herself that both of you survived that storm yesterday." He looked from one to the other. "Even the kids were praying for you." He started back to his office but turned to add, "And I didn't tell her about the engagement."

Ryan and Laurette stood hand in hand. "We're grateful for all the prayers that kept us safe," Laurette said softly. "I'll tell Diane about Ryan and me this afternoon."

"Fish-and-chips?" Ryan asked at the bottom of the stairs.

"What else?"

As they sat over lunch, Ryan told her, "I called my mother this morning. She says to give you a big hug. She can't wait to meet you." He picked up a piece of fish. "She also asked if she and Harvey could play at the wedding."

"They'll come to Sitka?" Rette put her glass down with a bang.

He smiled and nodded. "Said she wouldn't miss my wedding for anything." Laurette could see the joy in his eyes.

"I'm sure my parents will come, too. I think my mother's a little disappointed that I wanted to be married here, but she's already making plans."

"Are you sure you don't want to go home?"

She put her hand over his. "Sitka is home. I belong here with you."

twenty-one

There were many tasks to be taken care of the first day back at the SAM office. Laurette picked up a stack of messages and groaned, "Lots to do." She did take time to call Diane. "We'll come to dinner as soon as things settle down a bit. I'm going to be busy helping Ruth pack," she told her friend when Diane insisted they get together to start wedding plans.

She decided to stop at the grocery store for something quick to cook for dinner. When she opened the door into the kitchen, she found Ruth sitting at the table. "Are you waiting for supper?" Laurette asked her.

"Oh, you're home. I started a list of what I want to take with me." Ruth patted the pencil and paper in front of her.

"Not a very long list." Laurette saw a blank piece of paper.

"I don't know what I need. Will you help me?" Ruth looked like a lost child.

Laurette hugged her old friend and kissed her cheek. "Of course I will. I need to start supper right now, though. Ryan's coming to eat with us. Maybe he can help."

"I'll miss you reading to me at night," Ruth said wistfully.

"I'll come visit you, and we'll read together then."

"I'd like that." Ruth's sweet smile sent a wave of love through Laurette. "I'm glad you'll take care of my house."

"Ryan and I will live here when we're married."

"Are you getting married soon?"

"At Christmastime. And you must come to the wedding." Laurette had put the groceries away and started peeling potatoes.

By the time Ryan walked in the back door, pots were steaming on the stove and the table had been set. "Smells a lot better than the canned soup I fixed last night," he said, giving Laurette a kiss on the cheek. "And how is my favorite girlfriend?" he asked Ruth.

Laurette kept looking at her watch.

"You have a date?" Ryan asked as they cleared the dinner table.

"I told my mother I'd call at eight their time. She's to have my father in the house."

"Where does he usually spend the evening? Is there a ritual I should know about? Do I have to stay in the barn?" he teased.

"Sometimes I think my father would rather be in the barn than in front of the television. His farm is his life."

"Does he have a lot of animals in that barn?"

"No. Just a few chickens, but he loves to tinker on the farm machinery." She smiled as she washed a plate and handed it to him to dry. "That's why I learned to fix motors. It was one way I could get my dad's attention."

"What about your mother? Does she work on motors, too?"

"No. She cooks, sews, and reads a lot. It may not sound like a good marriage, but it is. They do a lot of things together, but they each have their own things to do as well."

"You're going to want your space. Is that what you're telling me?"

"I want to be with you as much as I can." She reached up to put soapsuds on the end of his nose. "Now let's go make that call." She picked up a towel to dry her hands and wipe his face.

A minute later, Laurette was saying, "Daddy, I want you to meet Ryan."

"So who is this guy who wants to steal my little girl?" Mr. Martel growled.

"I am not a little girl. I am twenty-three years old." Laurette rolled her eyes at Ryan.

"Good evening, Mr. Martel. I don't want to steal your daughter. I only want to ask for her hand in marriage."

"Isn't that nice, Fred? He's an old-fashioned boy to ask our permission," Laurette's mother said from the extension phone.

"Daddy, will you be part of my wedding and give me away?"

"I don't know if I want to give you away." The laughter in his voice gave away his gruff words.

Ryan smiled at Rette. "I could offer a lifetime supply of salmon in exchange for Laurette."

Mr. Martel's loud guffaw raced across the phone line. "You'll fit right into this family, Ryan. And I'll take that supply of salmon."

"Rette may have to catch them. She's a better fisherman than I am."

"Will you mind coming to Sitka in the winter?" Laurette asked. "It will be dark, wet, and cold."

"You'll be our sunshine, sweetheart," her mother answered.

"It's a good time for me," her father added. "I don't have a lot of farmwork in the winter."

"Who will stand up with you?" her mother asked.

"I've e-mailed Jenny. She's the one who talked me into coming to Sitka, and she went to school with Ryan. I have a flower girl and a ring bearer. They're the children of our boss."

"Sounds like you've made a lot of progress. Will you need my help?"

"Of course, Mom. I have no idea about what to wear. Maybe I'll have to fly down to look for a dress."

"I'll buy the ticket if you'll go shopping with your mother," her father offered. "Of course, I'll expect you to bring me some salmon."

"I'll smoke some for you," Ryan offered.

"Now that's an offer I can't refuse. I'm going to get off the phone and let the women talk. Nice to meet you, Ryan. Look forward to seeing you both. Love you, Rette. Let me know when you can fly home."

Ryan smiled at Rette and turned off his extension phone. She visited with her mother for another ten minutes. When she put the phone down and turned to him, he sat by Ruth with the Bible, reading to her.

"I've been replaced," she joked.

The three of them read and discussed the Scriptures until Ruth said she felt tired.

Left alone, the young couple sat holding hands and planning their future.

❧

The work at SAM continued at a brisk pace. Some cruise ships would keep stopping in Sitka until the middle of October. Most would move to southern waters sometime in September.

The silver salmon run started in late August. John needed to fish and appealed to Laurette. "Could you get Mother ready to move? I have the papers from the home telling her what she should bring."

"What about the house? Aren't there family things that should be packed for your children?"

"Thank you for thinking of them. I talked to my daughter, Marty, last night. She can't get away until the first of the year. I'll try to help you pack, and I do have a place to store things at my house until she can go through them. I know you'll want to change things so it's your home."

"I won't make any drastic changes for a while. I want Ruth to still feel like it's home when she comes to visit."

"I thank God for you every day. You've made our lives much easier. Mother loves you and has come to depend on you. I worried about what would happen when you left Sitka."

"I thank God He gave me a reason to stay," she replied.

Laurette spent hours helping Ruth go through clothes and decide what to keep. Her picture albums took days. Laurette framed pictures of Ruth's family to go on the wall of her new room. She would take her big chair and television. Ryan gave her a large print King James Bible and called it his housewarming gift when they helped John move her to the Pioneer Home.

A few days later Diane called to invite Ryan and Laurette to dinner. Rette moaned, "I haven't had any time to look for a job. Getting Ruth moved has taken all my spare time."

"Don't worry about it right now. Just come to dinner on Saturday. We're having a celebration."

"Did I miss a birthday?"

"No. Just come and be surprised."

"I don't know what she's up to. I wonder if this will turn out to be a wedding shower," Laurette fussed to Ryan.

"As long as there's food, I don't care," Ryan told her.

She poked him in the ribs. "Just like a man. Only thinks of his stomach."

"Speaking of dinner, you want to go out to eat tonight?"

"No thanks. I'm still trying to get our house settled."

"You've got months to do that," he protested.

"I hope to be working."

He grimaced. "Me, too, but so far I've had no response to my inquiries. I did have someone call about my offer to sell my trailer."

"We've agreed that the money from that will buy you a piano."

"Gives me an idea. If you won't go out with me, I'll go play at the Dockside Hotel tonight."

❧

Saturday, Ryan picked Laurette up at what would someday

be their home. "I bought some flowers for Diane."

"And I picked up some books for David and Katie."

The dinner was delicious and the company lively. "That mouse stays in the cage," Diane had insisted before they sat down.

"Do we get cake now, Mommy?" Katie asked, bouncing up and down.

Diane nodded as she cleared plates from the table. "I don't need help," she told Laurette. "Go sit by Ryan."

Ryan took Laurette's hand when she did as she was told. They watched as Diane brought a fancy cake to the table. Laurette gave Ryan a puzzled look as Diane put the cake in front of Tyler.

"This is Daddy's celebration," David said with a beaming face. "And we didn't tell, Mommy. We kept the secret."

"Yes, you did, and I'm proud of you." She stood behind her husband. "But I am more proud to announce that Tyler has been promoted."

"What's this?" Ryan asked.

"I've been promoted to the head office. I'll be taking a supervisory position," Tyler said quietly.

"That's wonderful. Will you still work the cruise ship side?"

"No. I'm going to handle freight."

"Now don't you two start talking shop," Diane scolded. "I want you to tell them the rest of the story, Tyler."

Tyler smiled at the young couple. "I've recommended you to take my place in Sitka," he told Ryan.

Laurette looked at Ryan's surprised face and reached up to touch his cheek. "An answer to prayer?"

He nodded and put his arm around her shoulders. "A full-time job." His voice held wonder as he pulled her close to him.

"How soon do you move?" Laurette asked Diane.

"Tyler is supposed to start in Ketchikan the first of December." She held up her hand. "But we'll be here for your wedding.

We have to sell this house and find one to move into. I don't think the kids and I will move until the first of the year. Now I have a question for you."

Laurette wondered what else could happen.

"I'm going to be quitting my job, and I'd like you to consider taking over."

"I told you I don't know how to teach school."

"We'll talk about that. You don't need a teaching certificate, and the curriculum is all set up. You just monitor the kids' progress as they go through the workbooks. You can do it," Diane insisted.

"I think she should do it," Ryan stated, pulling Rette close to him. "It would be better than waiting on tables," he told her.

"Could we have our cake now?" Katie demanded.

"So many decisions. It makes my mind whirl," Laurette told Diane when she thanked her friend for a pleasant evening. She carried a piece of cake on a plate to share with Ryan later.

"You'd make a good teacher," Diane told her friend.

Ryan and Laurette sat in his Volkswagen and talked a long time that evening. "The Lord has been good to us. You told me to put my trust in Jesus, and He would guide us. And I think He has put the teaching job in front of you for a reason. I'd like you to think about it," Ryan told Laurette. "You're good with kids. You can do it."

"There aren't many students enrolled. I'd have to supervise two or three grades."

"Think about it." He brushed the hair back from her face.

"What will your job be in the winter?"

"I may have to go to Ketchikan a few times. We'll be setting up schedules with the cruise lines for next year."

He gave her a hug. "Will you work for me next summer?"

"As long as we have time to go fishing. Have to keep my father happy."

He cupped her chin in his hand. "It's time I let you get some sleep." She could read the unspoken feelings in his eyes before he kissed her good night.

❧

On Sunday Laurette took time off from tasks at work to meet Diane at church. She had trouble keeping her mind on the sermon. She kept thinking how the sanctuary would look decorated for her wedding.

When the pastor invited anyone in the congregation to come forward, she had turned to whisper to Diane. She saw Diane's eyes grow wide and felt her friend poke her shoulder. Looking at where her friend pointed, she caught her breath.

Ryan, dressed in his SAM jacket and pressed jeans, with his head held high, walked to the altar rail. He knelt before the waiting pastor and spoke in a strong voice. "I became a Christian as a child, but I only recently learned what it means to live as one. Today I recommit my life to Jesus Christ and ask Him to remain in my heart and guide my ways from this day forward."

Tears of pride and joy spilled down Laurette's cheeks. *Love is the reason behind everything You do, Lord. Thank You.*

A Letter To Our Readers

Dear Reader:

In order that we might better contribute to your reading enjoyment, we would appreciate your taking a few minutes to respond to the following questions. We welcome your comments and read each form and letter we receive. When completed, please return to the following:

Fiction Editor
Heartsong Presents
PO Box 719
Uhrichsville, Ohio 44683

1. Did you enjoy reading *Alaskan Summer* by Marilou H. Flinkman?
   ☐ Very much! I would like to see more books by this author!
   ☐ Moderately. I would have enjoyed it more if

   _____

   _____

   _____

2. Are you a member of **Heartsong Presents**? ☐ Yes ☐ No
   If no, where did you purchase this book? _____

   _____

3. How would you rate, on a scale from 1 (poor) to 5 (superior), the cover design? _____

4. On a scale from 1 (poor) to 10 (superior), please rate the following elements.

   ____ Heroine   ____ Plot
   ____ Hero   ____ Inspirational theme
   ____ Setting   ____ Secondary characters

5. These characters were special because? _____

_____

_____

6. How has this book inspired your life? _____

_____

_____

7. What settings would you like to see covered in future
   Heartsong Presents books? _____

_____

_____

8. What are some inspirational themes you would like to see
   treated in future books? _____

_____

_____

9. Would you be interested in reading other **Heartsong
   Presents** titles? ❑ Yes ❑ No

10. Please check your age range:
    ❑ Under 18   ❑ 18-24
    ❑ 25-34   ❑ 35-45
    ❑ 46-55   ❑ Over 55

Name_____

Occupation _____

Address _____

City, State, Zip_____

Oregon Breeze

4 stories in 1

*F*eeling trapped by the way life has boxed them in, four Oregonians step out to embrace new challenges. Will a small step of faith free these lonely hearts to love completely? Or will circumstances bind them to the past?

Titles by author Birdie L. Etchison include: *Finding Courtney*, *The Sea Beckons*, *Ring of Hope*, and *Woodhaven Acres*.

Contemporary, paperback, 480 pages, 5³/₁₆" x 8"

—————————————————————

Presents

Great Inspirational Romance at a Great Price!

Heartsong Presents books are inspirational romances in
contemporary and historical settings, designed to give you an
enjoyable, spirit-lifting reading experience. You can choose
wonderfully written titles from some of today's best authors like
Hannah Alexander, Andrea Boeshaar, Yvonne Lehman, Tracie
Peterson, and many others.

When ordering quantities less than twelve, above titles are $2.97 each.
Not all titles may be available at time of order.